Megan Besing's addition to the Chasing Fire: Montana series is a rousing success. Brimming with tension, romance, mystery, and danger, Flashover keeps you on the edge of your seat the entire way through. I guarantee after reading this one, you will be itching to dive into the rest of the series!

KATHRYN, GOODREADS

Flashover is the second book in the Chasing Fire: Montana series, and it was filled with just as much action and excitement as the first! This book was a beautiful reminder of redemption and hope.

COURTNEY, GOODREADS

Exciting from beginning to end and full of quotable moments! One of my favorite's was "Don't let yourself think that you can mess up so much that you can ruin God's plans." An excellent reminder to think more of God's ways than ours. Wonderful characters! Sophie was brave and compassionate. Houston was a swoon-worthy hero who didn't know how great he was.

NOELLE, GOODREADS

This is a fast moving thriller that explores how our pasts can affect our future and how God is in control. Excellent characters and exciting action highlight this story.

What an awesome read. *Flashover* has danger, action, second chances, horses, and unexpected surprises as Houston and Sophie must fight to survive the external threats. You don't want to miss this gripping romantic suspense story involving redemption and second chances.

This Christian romantic suspense is nonstop action and suspense from page one. A harrowing second chance with horses, fire, wayward children, and searching for God's will and provision. I couldn't put this book down. Indeed, I quite literally blazed through and it held my attention firmly. It was a great addition to this series and I cannot wait until the next book comes out! This was my first by this author but I'm looking forward to checking out more by her soon.

FLASHOVER

CHASING FIRE: MONTANA | BOOK 2

A SERIES CREATED BY SUSAN MAY WARREN AND LISA PHILLIPS

MEGAN BESING

Flashover

Chasing Fire: Montana, Book 2

Copyright © 2023 Sunrise Media Group LLC

Print ISBN: 978-1-953783-XX-X

eBook ISBN: 978-1-953783-XX-X

For more information about Megan Besing, please contact the author via her website: meganbesing.com

Published in the United States of America

Cover Design: Susan Warren Creative

sunrise
PUBLISHING

Flashover
Chasing Fire: Montana, Book 2
Copyright © 2024 Sunrise Media Group LLC
Print ISBN: 978-1-963372-11-3
Ebook ISBN: 978-1-963372-10-6

All Scripture quotations, unless otherwise indicated, are taken from
the King James Version.

For more information about Megan Besing, please access the
author's website at meganbesing.com.

Published in the United States of America.
Cover Design: Lynnette Bonner

To my favorite daughter, I love you.
What a joy it is to be your mother.
Oh, sweet one, always run to Him.

The name of the Lord is a strong tower;
the righteous run to it and are safe.
Proverbs 18:10 NIV

Though Satan should buffet,
Though trials should come,
Let this blest assurance control.
That Christ has regarded my helpless estate,
And hath shed His own blood for my soul.

ONE

SOPHIE LAMB SHOULD'VE NEVER SAID YES. NOW she would have to stand here and watch someone get killed riding one of her horses.

The sunrise soared over the roofs of the staged western town and glistened on the camera screens, which failed to catch the scent of ash in the air or the two-week-old wildfire smoke still swelling behind them. Unlike the hushed crowd around her, Sophie wasn't there to get a peek at Hollywood's latest stars reshooting a scene. She was there mainly for Thunderbolt. Her most cantankerous black stallion. The one she'd for sure advised the director not to use.

"And…action."

At the director's command, Sophie curled her toes in the pointed ends of her dusty cowboy boots. *Come on, boy. Just one good take.*

Thunderbolt's rider, the recently upgraded extra named Jonah, leaned forward in his saddle. Holding on to his Stetson with one hand and the reins in the other, he had Thunderbolt galloping in hot. Too hot. A trail of dust paraded behind as Thunderbolt's hooves pounded the dry ground. The clouded air

1

tickled Sophie's throat, but she dared not make a sound to ruin the take.

They flew past the trading post, then the church. Another few heartbeats and they'd reach their mark beside two of her other horses tied to a wooden post out in front of the set's bank.

Sophie squeezed past one of the production assistants sipping coffee and zeroed in on Thunderbolt's movements. His front leg had healed quicker than Sophie's weak ankle, but he still needed slow and steady just as they'd practiced a million times before everything blew up on set the two weeks before.

Literally.

But Thunderbolt's ears weren't pulled back. He wasn't groaning. Wasn't limping.

Sophie slowed her own gait and slipped in behind one of the assistant directors in the front row of the crowd.

Maybe this speed and paired rider would work. For one take.

Jonah yanked back on the reins. Hard. Thunderbolt stopped ten feet from the desired mark. Dust swirled and went straight for the other actors, making Kathryn Canary, the lead actress, cough.

"Cut!" Cosmos Ferguson, the director, stomped toward the filming scene. "Jonah! Didn't I tell you to pull up closer to the other horses? This should have taken one take."

Jonah dropped the reins onto his lap and lifted his hands. "You think this stupid thing listens to me?"

Sophie scowled. Great. She'd been assured Jonah was an experienced rider. Thunderbolt snorted and lifted his right front leg. Sophie pushed back her shoulders and marched across the boundary line toward Jonah.

However, Cosmos intercepted her. "Problem?"

In front of Sophie, Jonah fanned his face with his stiff Stetson as he laughed loudly into his cell phone.

Thunderbolt's left ear twitched.

Sophie nodded her head in the direction of Thunderbolt and Jonah. "That pairing is never going to work. However, I think Jonah could ride Pudding or even Chestnut. Goldie too if—"

Cosmos held up his palm. "Jonah's character must be on the darkest horse. The animal he rides is more than his transportation. It's the outer expression of the story's mood at this point of the movie."

No character's mood was worth Thunderbolt getting hurt. Or worse. He'd already been through enough trauma before she'd rescued him. All her horses had in one way or another deserved a better life. "Right. I understand that. Except..."

From on top of Thunderbolt, Jonah moved his arm through the air to something he said over his phone, and his hat flew out of his grip. The Stetson twisted into the air and dropped. But gravity didn't allow it to simply land on the ground. That would have been too easy.

Instead, it smacked against Thunderbolt's lifted leg.

He released a neigh. He reared back, eyes wide and ears flat.

Not again.

Sophie raised her hands. "Whoa, Thunderbolt. Easy."

But the only easy thing about the morning so far had been arriving on time.

The horse shot off, derby race style. Jonah hollered. His fingers reached for the reins but missed as he clung to his phone. His feet bucked in the air, as his boots weren't in the stirrups. The man couldn't even pretend to be a cowboy. "Someone stop this thing!"

If only Sophie could have pulled both of her horse trailers here and brought Daisy and Frank along too. Even Peanut. Then she could have galloped after Thunderbolt and Jonah.

Sophie put her fingers in her mouth and whistled. Thunderbolt twisted his ears back but sprinted on through the opening between two wooden set buildings.

Spencer Storm, one of the actors off scene, spurred Sophie's horse Goldie into action and took off after Thunderbolt. At least someone hadn't lied about his horse experience. Once he caught up to the pair, he grabbed Thunderbolt's reins and steered everyone back toward the cheering crowd.

As Sophie ran to intercept, Jonah yelled something, but Sophie's gaze snagged on a man wearing a navy baseball cap who walked behind the set's bank building.

She stutter-stepped, and it had nothing to do with her old ankle injuries.

The man's height resembled her brother's. So did his dark hair and nose profile.

"Crispin."

But the man didn't stop.

She took two steps after him. "Crispin!"

The man's shoulders seemed about the same size as Crispin's. Though, the closer she got, the more he looked different from her memories. Too thin. He had a beard and wore cargo pants. Maybe it wasn't her brother. But then again, anyone could change in three years.

She sure had.

Once more, he didn't stop, and what was she thinking? Her brother had been declared dead. Even if she didn't believe it. No matter that Homeland Security kept affirming it. Regardless of what she believed, her special ops brother wasn't going to show up on the set of a movie. She didn't have the power to wish him or anyone into existence.

However, it seemed her heart, rather than her head, was in control of her feet as she jogged in the man's direction until Jonah and Spencer rode up.

Red faced, Jonah spat. He jumped down from Thunderbolt and blocked her view. "Your horse tried to kill me."

Her fingers fisted, and she bit back a retort to Jonah while her gaze returned to the alleyway. It was empty.

She swallowed a longing that surprised her. Clearly, deep inside she still clung to a fragment of hope that her brother was alive.

Cosmos marched up beside Jonah and folded his arms. "Your hat spooked this horse, and I don't believe cell phones are props for any of our western scenes."

Jonah had the decency to look guilty.

The director didn't ease his glare. "You either ride a horse, or you're out of my movie. I don't care that my godfather owes your great-aunt a favor."

Jonah held the director's gaze for three of Sophie's thundering heartbeats before he said, "Not. That. One."

Poor Thunderbolt. It wasn't his fault. Sophie could load up all her horses and be done with the stress. But she wanted to be able to rescue more horses one day. Needed enough money to build five more barns. Or at least the one she had her bank loan application in for. For that, she needed this gig.

She slid next to Spencer and took Thunderbolt's reins from the movie star. "Thank you so much. I'm so sorry. Thunderbolt likes to run from his problems."

The slightest smile lit up Spencer's face. "Been there, done that. In fact, it was pretty much just a couple weeks ago."

Sophie nodded. "I heard about that."

According to rumors around the town of Ember, Spencer's now girlfriend, a hotshot firefighter, had been kidnapped and tied up in a burning house. But then again, rumors could spread quicker than the forest fire blazing in the distance. Sophie's past was proof of that.

Jonah grunted.

Sophie stroked Thunderbolt's cheek and then ran her palm down his leg. Nothing appeared broken, other than her latest attempt at fundraising for the ranch.

She took a deep breath. She should have also brought Daisy from the beginning, but she hated leaving Peanut and Frank alone at the barn. "I have one more horse back at the ranch that might work. Daisy is mostly black. Has white markings on her head and two spots on her feet."

Cosmos studied Jonah. "Can Daisy handle a rider who *will* listen better to your instructions?"

Jonah snarled but didn't deny anything.

"Daisy was a trail horse. She has a good and

patient temperament." Maybe a bit too dormant. When her owner passed, his son assumed there was something wrong with the aged horse and had wanted to ship her off to a meat-processing facility in Mexico. Sophie had gotten a tip about the transaction and drove hours to bring the malnourished horse safely to her ranch.

Cosmos checked his watch. "If the weather and fire cooperate, we'll need Daisy here as soon as possible. We were already supposed to be heading to the backlot by now. I'll make sure someone who knows what they're doing looks after Pudding and Chestnut and the rest of your horses at the set livery while you're gone."

"That would be great."

She spotted another familiar face behind the director. This time, her eyes weren't playing tricks on her. A pile of auburn curls and a hot pink headband sat on top of Marley's head. Her best friend carried an arrangement of flowers that seemed almost as heavy as Thunderbolt's saddle. Marley's oversized overall pants rubbed together as she walked, making whooshing sounds that harmonized with the water sloshing around in the glass vase in her arms.

When Marley spotted Sophie, her smile matched the cheerfulness of the yellow roses amongst the green foliage, which Marley always called the backdrop for the flower stars. "Do you know where *the* Kathryn Canary is?"

Sophie glanced over her shoulder for the actress. Her gaze snagged once more on the empty alleyway set beside the bank and then moved on toward the vacant casting chairs. "Maybe try her dressing room?

Or I think I saw her assistant over by the food table before the last take."

Marley's eyes lit up over the top layer of roses. "An assistant would be way less intimidating."

Sophie bumped her shoulder into Marley's as they headed in the direction of both the food and livery. "Now's the perfect time to meet your favorite actress. What have I told you—"

"Yes, yes, movie stars are people too, I know. But knowing that still doesn't make my words stop stuttering. I'm just glad you're still here. I wish I'd known though; I would have brought you a smoothie."

Thunderbolt blew out a breath, and Sophie patted his side as they walked. "Thanks for the thought, nonetheless. This one is in timeout, and I've got to go get Daisy."

Marley wrinkled her nose, causing her freckles to bunch together. "Thunderbolt, you need to stop being a stinker. But everyone will love to meet sweet Daisy. I still can't believe someone would send her to the glue factory."

Sophie put her hands over Thunderbolt's ears. "We don't say G.L.U.E. around the horses."

Marley laughed until her smile slipped away as they neared the food table where a group of extras dressed as cowboys pointed to the sky behind Thunderbolt.

Sophie turned along with Marley. Smoke soared above the tree line, blocking the mountain view in the distance.

Marley shifted the vase of flowers. "Hope they get the fire under control soon."

"I'm sure the firefighters will." They had to. Her

ranch wasn't too far from where the fire had been heading the past few days.

A laugh floated over to them from one of the massive production trailers with a door marked "wardrobe department." Kathyrn tucked a section of her blonde hair behind her ear as she spoke to her assistant.

Sophie nodded toward the women. "In case you didn't know, Kathryn Canary is the one in the pink dress. Her assistant is in the jeans."

"Thanks, girl. Be safe driving back. Call me later. We'll set dinner plans, complete with smoothies."

"Perfect." Sophie waved bye and weaved Thunderbolt around a section of lighting and props. As she neared her horse trailer parked beside the livery barn, a red convertible blocked her hitch. She would have sighed if it would have done any good. Instead, she glanced back to the parking lot. At least her truck wasn't blocked in. She'd have to use her old trailer at home to bring Daisy back.

She pulled Thunderbolt toward the outside corral. "Looks like you're not coming home with me quite yet, boy."

A flash of blue over her shoulder in the parking lot stole Sophie's attention. A man holding an orange — one of her brother's favorite fruits — and a cell phone stood beside the Kalispell Sound and Light semi-truck.

"Crispin." Her voice came out shakier than the yell she intended.

The man paused.

Sophie stopped walking, and Thunderbolt's nose bumped into her. But the man in the navy T-shirt simply offered her a chin nod, slid his phone in his pocket, and peeled his orange before hopping into the truck. Perhaps she'd gotten less sleep than she thought last night, worrying about the smell of smoke lingering in the air when she had locked up her barn. The man was probably a film set worker.

Of course he was.

Thunderbolt snorted.

Sophie clicked her tongue and tugged his leads forward toward the set livery. "Yes, you're right, a little scenery change will do me good. And you better be on your best behavior while I fetch Daisy."

She needed to stop hoping. She couldn't keep wishing to change the past. Even if today was the third anniversary of her brother's supposed death.

Hotshot Houston James knew firsthand that fire played by its own rules.

The tops of the Ponderosa Pines bent toward the east at the crest of the hill as the wind hinted at today's fire travel plans—and the fact the weatherman's Red Flag Warning had been correct. With the persistent wildfire ever greedy, if Jude County Hotshots didn't finish the protective trench along the sloped area and clear the debris, the land—and lives—in the valley were at risk.

Houston sank his Pulaski fire ax into the dirt. The sharpened point struck a tree root. He heaved out a breath and adjusted his collar that rubbed against the scarred skin around his neck. There was no time to take in the rolling areas of lush trees behind him. The brush and growing saplings under the towering pines had been removed and placed outside of the firebreak.

A piece of ash landed on his lip and tasted like bitter disaster.

With a grunt, he wiped his mouth and heaved his Pulaski all the way through the root. The crack echoed in accord with his fellow crew members, Charlie Benning and Orion Price, as they flanked each side, trenching out the best fire line. Anything less and the ranch just on the edge of the basin with its dry grazing field, had no hope of surviving the fire raging toward it.

Not a single hawk screeched in the smokiness above. No woodpecker drummed against a tree destined for destruction. Nothing over the rumble of the chainsaws up closer to the fire, clearing out for the firebreak. Yet another sound in the woods made Houston freeze mid swing.

Laughter.

His back twinged as he used the forward motion to twist around instead of striking the ground. There was nothing funny about saving someone's property. Someone's life. No hotshot would dare to find trench work humorous, which meant more trouble.

One day people might realize how much they put others in danger when they ignored evacuation orders.

A series of popping noises echoed in the distance and then more laughter rang from behind the trenching line.

Houston pointed back and to their left. "You guys hear that?"

Charlie finished the swing of his Pulaski and tilted his head. "Not quite gunshots."

"Worse." At least it was for a dry day like today.

Houston turned toward Orion. "Price, I think someone's setting off firecrackers."

Orion might be close to fifteen years younger, but with this being Houston's first year as a hotshot, or even as a firefighter, Orion, the second youngest member, nicknamed Ry, held seniority.

Orion grabbed his radio. "Chief, we've got some suspicious activity back here. Possibly some people setting off firecrackers, of all things."

Their Chief, Conner Young, was located closer to the fire along with the two women on the crew. The other four guys—who everyone had dubbed 'the Trouble Boys' were further away down the line. "Take James with you. Report back."

Houston took a chug of water and frowned down at his steel-toed boots.

Jogging over, Orion thumped Charlie on the back. "You sure you can handle this trench alone old man?"

Charlie laughed. "By the time you return, a line from here to the Canadian border will be trenched. You just worry about James outrunning you."

Houston slipped his ax into his pack and double-timed it toward the trail. The laughter had come maybe thirty yards away, downhill. Orion was only a few paces behind him when another pop splintered through the air. It almost resonated like a gunshot until a round of crackling pops followed. Definitely firecrackers.

Houston slowed his steps and put up his hand. Orion crept up behind him.

In front of them on a plateau area, surrounded by a grouping of Lodgepole Pines that may not survive another day depending on the fire's path, were three teens. Two older. One younger. All within the same age groups of the boys who had been in Houston's old youth group.

The blond wore a white T-shirt with cut-off sleeves and had more freckles than muscles. He ran his thumb over a lighter in his hand and lit a firecracker, then threw it at a decaying tree with a hole in its center.

The firecracker ricocheted off the bark and nearly exploded back into the teens' faces.

The tallest one had his head shaved, but it wasn't just the cigarette sticking out of his mouth that snagged Houston's attention, but rather the black caterpillar-type mustache gracing his upper lip. He blew out a bluff of smoke and then threw the stick in his hand at the boy who missed. "Preston, if you miss again—"

"Shut up, Finn." Preston spat. "I won't. Just hand me another firecracker."

The baby-faced boy sported camo cargo pants that didn't match his brand-new red tennis shoes. He sat on a stump with a smirk on his face but remained quiet.

Houston stepped forward. "Are you out of your mind? There's a fire raging a mile from here that could take out this entire forest, and you're lighting firecrackers?" He marched forward until he held out his hand in front of Preston's chest. "Hand over that lighter. You were supposed to have evacuated this area."

None of the boys moved, except Finn, Mr. Mustache, who'd thrown the stick. He swayed his head back and forth like a snake preparing to strike. "You aren't his father. And you ain't mine."

"Hand over the lighter." Orion came up beside Houston. "Do you know how much more damage you could have caused?"

"Just having a little fun." Preston shrugged.

Finn smirked. "They're only baby squirrels."

Houston locked his gaze onto Finn. "You're lighting firecrackers in a drought, and you're trying to hurt animals?"

Finn's mustache almost curled up with his gummy grin as he took the cigarette away from his mouth. "I'm guessing it was a firecracker that carved up your skin."

Finn's remark about his burned body shouldn't have mattered, but it made Houston rock back on his heels.

Preston spat on the ground and crossed his arms. "Nah, he was probably always that ugly."

There was no remorse in either of the two teens' eyes, but Houston didn't have a chance to check out the silent one who had taken a few steps backward.

Houston lunged and grabbed the lighter. He secured it in his palm.

Preston scoffed, "Hey!" He reached for the lighter while his freckles on his nose grew red. "Harassment much?"

Houston slid the lighter into his pocket.

"Hardly." Orion growled as he hooked his thumb back toward their crew's fire line. "All of you, get to walking. You ignored an evacuation order for this area. We'll see if the sheriff thinks you need to take the fire safety class at Wildlands Academy."

Preston puffed out his chest and turned toward Orion. "You can't make us do nothing."

Finn pulled out a string of firecrackers he must

have somehow lit behind his back with his cigarette. "Now!" He flung it right at Houston.

Houston swatted the firecrackers to the ground. The lit fuse singed the tip of his pinky. He squeezed his burned finger into a fist. Pops thundered against the creaking trees.

The boys scrambled away with Orion hot on Finn's tail. Houston chased after them. There had been no firefighter training for any of this, but if he and Orion worked together, they could get Finn, the ringleader. The others would follow.

Except another noise canceled Houston's plan. An engine started.

Houston skidded to a stop. The quiet boy sat on top of a camouflaged four-wheeler that must have been parked behind an overgrowth of bushes.

Houston pivoted and ran faster. Harder. If only he didn't have his pack still on. But a hotshot never left his pack.

The boy gunned the four-wheeler. The engine roared, and he shifted, reaching Preston before Houston could even lunge for the kid.

Preston waved his arms at the quiet one. "Move, Lewis."

Lewis scooted to the back of the four-wheeler. Preston hopped on and spun the wheels, dirt and dried leaves spit into the air. They did a one-eighty and aimed right for their ringleader, who Orion had grabbed, Finn's shirt fisted in his hand.

Preston shifted into third gear. Lewis clung to the back bars under the rack. Houston tucked his chin and dashed after them. But the four-wheeler blazed away. Aimed right toward Orion.

"Stop!" Houston yelled.

But the boy shifted up a gear.

"Price!"

Right before contact, Orion jumped behind a tree. Finn yanked away from Orion, latched arms with Lewis on the back, and jumped up. All three of the boys rumbled away through the woods.

Orion heaved out a breath. "If I ever mention criminal justice as a career, remind me juvenile delinquents aren't my thing."

Houston sent a glare skyward. Working with juveniles, period, wasn't his thing either. Not anymore. God had made sure of that when He took away Houston's youth pastor position and gave it to someone else.

Orion pushed himself off the ground, but his eyes widened at something behind Houston.

A waft of smoke hit Houston's nose. He fisted his hands.

Houston peered over his shoulders. Flames. Hot and angry. Devouring the leaves, fallen branches, and pine needles on the ground.

Orion sprinted for the hungry fire. "The firecrackers or his cigarette flamed up against the dry brush. It's spreading. We've got to get it out now."

Houston opened his pack and pulled out his shovel.

As the heat hit Houston's healed skin, the past rushed back to him.

Orion heaped dirt onto the flames. "Dude, come on."

Move.

But Houston couldn't. Face to face with the fire moving fast, he couldn't do anything. His heart thumped in his chest. His eyes locked on the shovel handle. Not on the ashes. The heat. Or anything that reminded him of the day that changed his life. His childhood home that almost burned to the ground with him inside.

Orion stomped his boot on another spark of flaming pine cone. "Whatever that was, don't let Captain see it happen again."

Houston swallowed, and his throat burned with smoke. How did Houston ever think he could be a hotshot firefighter?

TWO

THERE WAS FAR TOO MUCH SMOKE CASCADING down the tree-lined hillside. Maybe it had been a good thing Thunderbolt had misbehaved. Sophie would just load up the rest of her animals. They didn't need to be breathing in this soot-laced air.

As she drove under the arched iron sign that spelled out her inherited ranch's name, something moved on her porch. A man stood by her front door.

Of course today was the moment the bank's loan department would finally be taking Sophie's application to build more barns seriously.

Shifting her truck into neutral, she set the brake. Now was not the time for a visitor—she needed to get her horses out of here.

Except the man wasn't wearing a suit.

She threw her truck door open. "Can I help you?"

The man finally turned. Blue eyes. Brown hair greased back.

His leathery, tanned face was at least twenty years older. A spotty beard supported a variety of white and gray along with its reddish-brown mixture which didn't match the chestnut color poking out of his gray T-shirt. His tarnished, rounded work boots thumped against each of her porch steps. "This Valley Ranch?"

His voice had a strained quality that didn't exactly sound welcoming.

There was something off about this guy. And she wasn't about to tell him anything. "You looking for someone?"

He spat on the ground and tipped his chin toward the side of her house. "I pulled in looking for Lewy. My bike is parked over yonder. Think my gas gauge must be broken. It started to stall about a mile out, so I thought he'd spot me some gas to get me back into town."

"You're a friend of…Lewy's?" Marley's nephew, the teen who Sophie had been encouraged to offer a job, hadn't been here in weeks. Sophie's gaze went to the side of the porch, and she leaned closer to her own truck. The back of a motorcycle tire came into view on the other side of her house.

The man adjusted his belt buckle. "Yeah, I parked over there because I figured Lewy would have been back at the horse barn and all."

No matter if he was looking for Lewis or not, a stranger *should* have parked at the front of the house, especially with the lack of gas. What did the man really want?

Even while he held her gaze, she didn't miss the way his fingers tapped against his leg. Something wasn't quite right with his story.

She inspected his bootcut jeans and his jean jacket. "How do you know Lewis Truitt?"

His gaze shifted over her shoulder, toward the hazy woods and then whipped back to hers. "I'm sort of mentoring the kid. He needs some, shall we say, *molding.*"

Sophie doubted this man would earn any stickers as a mentor.

He spat again and ran the edge of his boot over the chew-laced dirt. "But he's proving to have some potential."

Sophie took a step back. "I wish I would have seen more of that potential while he'd been here. But I'm sorry to say Lewis hasn't worked here for a month."

Forgetting to brush down Daisy was one thing, stealing two hundred dollars from Sophie's kitchen crock was something else altogether.

She should have fired him after she'd caught him yelling at Peanut. However, she'd been trying to provide the second chance her friend Marley needed Lewis, her nephew and temporary ward, to have. Plus, Peanut wasn't exactly an obedient mule.

"I hadn't been told that." The man clenched his jaw but then flashed a grin wide enough to reveal a missing back tooth. "So, about that gas? Don't want to get stuck out here with the smoke rolling in. I heard they were evacuating the area. Hope you have someplace to wait out the fire."

She retreated and swiped her cell phone off the dash of her truck. Her location wasn't any of his concern. "It will only take a moment to grab the gas can from the shed." And get this man on his way— away from her. "I'll meet you at your bike."

Except he ignored his beat-up Harley and matched each of her steps toward the white shed, catty-corner to her barn.

She quickened her pace. "You're from Ember?"

"I'm there more often than not these days."

Not really an answer. She rotated her phone in her hand and slid her thumb over the unlocked screen.

"Always be ready. For anything." Her brother's warning flashed in her head, the one he'd given her before he headed away on his first assignment, an undercover mission. He wasn't even supposed to tell her that much about what he did for Homeland Security. But they had been the only person they each had left to depend on.

"Just in case, Lamby. Be ready." The nickname her brother adopted for her after she became obsessed with a cartoon about two sheep siblings had stuck. In response, she had started calling him Crispin after the oldest sheep. It had helped that Crispin hated his first name. *"People often hide their true motivations."*

Aw, now she had Crispin on the brain. Again.

She eyed the stranger out of the corner of her vision and slid the shed door wider with her hip. Walking inside, never turning her back to him, she picked up the red, plastic gas container.

"Here, let me get that." With two long strides, his rough hand landed on hers and tugged the gas can out of her grip.

She didn't even have time to suck in a breath before he marched away for his bike. Maybe the man really was only having a bad day.

Evacuation. Probably she needed to call the fire department and check on the status. She didn't want to leave her dream property and potentially never see its buildings standing again.

Stupid fire.

God had given her this place as a fresh start. So why was He going to take it all away now?

As he unscrewed the gas cap on his motorcycle, his elbow pushed back a section of his jacket. A gun, tucked between his shirt and his jeans, made her bite down on her tongue.

Maybe she'd start with a call to the sheriff.

Sophie pressed against the door of the shed. A holstered gun was one thing. Even a normal thing in this area. She kept one in her closet. But one stuffed in a temporary position meant he'd probably shoved it there in a hurry. To hide it from whoever might see. Someone like her when she arrived home.

Her fingers tightened around her phone. Before she could process what to do next, he'd already taken the gas spout out of his motorcycle.

As he held out the gas can, his eyes snapped to hers. "Seems like a lot of ranch for one little lady. Hope you have a man around. Maybe a father, or a brother, or another hired hand since Lewy didn't work out?"

Sophie took the offered gas container and then moved on the other side of the back tire, putting the motorcycle between her and the stranger. The man did not need any further information on her. "Hope the gas fixes your bike's problems."

With a tsk, he hiked his leg over his bike and shoved away the kickstand with his boot.

The deep throttle of the engine wasn't the only thing rattling in Sophie's chest. So many questions popped into her head, but her brother's advice so long ago took center stage.

"Sometimes questions are good." Crispin placed his hands on either side of her cheeks. "And sometimes questions cause

trouble. If something ever doesn't feel right, you get away as fast as you can. You promise me."

She nodded.

Crispin raised one of his brows.

With a sigh, she said, "I promise."

Her brother may have broken his word to her about his return, but Sophie would keep hers.

She pressed on a closed-lipped smile. "Be careful getting back with the fire and everything. The smoke can limit vision on the road quickly."

He saluted her with two fingers. "Might want to check those fire alerts yourself. You've been mighty helpful, little Lamb," he said with a wink.

He lifted his boots off the ground and sped off down her driveway. Even with the threat of an evacuation ticking away, she kept her focus on the road until she couldn't hear the roar of his engine.

"Little Lamb."

Had the stranger known her as Sophie *Lamb*, like the rest of the town of Ember?

Or as Rachel Tucker, whose brother nicknamed her *Lamby*. A name that needed to stay in the past.

Her phone beeped. The screen revealed her fears —an evacuation notice. Her gaze locked onto the hazy trees in the distance. More than just smoke was coming for her dream.

He only needed a little space from his memories. Then he'd be fine.

The teens were long gone, but the aftermath of their actions lived on. Including Houston's hesitation.

Something he couldn't let happen again.

Houston squeezed the handle in his hands and tossed dirt on the taunting coals.

Orion stood on the opposite boundary of the five square feet of the smoldering mess, raking in the dirt and snuffing out the occasional sparking pine cone. He cleared his throat. "James, you okay?"

But before Orion finished, their radios buzzed, and their chief came over the line. "I know you're still watching your fire there, but there's an evacuation order by the sheriff. I need one of you to do an evacuation check on a ranch. It's about half a mile south of your GPS location. Aerial spotted a truck headed there. It hasn't left yet. And the fire's pushing that way hard."

Houston took a step back from the heat. "I can go."

Orion's gaze shot across the smoke and pierced into Houston.

Once again, Orion pressed his lips together, and finally, he said into his radio, "James could gain some experience with an evacuation check."

"As long as it gets done." At the chief's response, Houston let out the breath he'd been holding. "Be quick. The flames aren't messing around today."

They never do.

Orion wiped his brow with his forearm. "Copy. I'll be wrapping it up here shortly and heading back to the line to help Benning."

Houston broke down his shovel and shoved it into his pack. "First the teens. Now evacuation round up. Not exactly how I saw our day going."

"Always got to be on our toes. Go get your head clear so we can end this fire. When we get back to HQ, we'll need to talk about your hesitation with the flames." Orion grimaced. "Can't imagine what you've been through. But we've got to be able to depend on you."

The weight of more than just the pack on his back seemed to hover on Houston. He couldn't fail. "And you can depend on me." He nodded as he tightened the straps over his shoulder. "After we destroy this fire, we can talk."

By then there would be no need to talk about Houston's hesitation. God wouldn't have opened the door for him to become a firefighter if Houston couldn't handle the position.

Right, God?

The jog through the woods stretched out Houston's coiled muscles. As he hurdled over a downed log, he hummed the chorus the kids would request Houston to play on his guitar for the Wednesday class. It didn't matter how old the hymn was. The words to "It Is Well" still were applicable no matter the generation singing. And especially to Houston.

Soon a valley snuck up below, where a white house with pale blue shutters was sandwiched between a winding rock driveway and a barn complete with a corral. A few sheds were lined up behind the house and a rectangular, open field anchored the end of the property. On the other side of the valley, another rolling hill of forest walled in the ranch. Up ahead, almost hidden due to the thickness of the pines on the other side of the road, far in the distance, a silver water tower poked up through the treetops on the opposite crest. Lettering on the side had faded beyond recognition other than the letter "E."

Houston's boots crunched against the ground as he marched down the dry, grassy incline. There was no vehicle in sight at the ranch. Hopefully, aerial only missed the owners leaving.

He took the porch steps two at a time and then banged on the front door. No footsteps. No shuffling noises from inside the house. Nothing but his own heartbeat.

After a few seconds, he knocked on the bay window beside the door. "I'm Jude County Hotshot Houston James. Is anyone—"

An odd screech had him walking to the edge of the porch and gawking toward the barn.

That brash shout mixed with the scraping of metal sounded like trouble. Whether animal, owner, or more than likely, both.

Houston jumped down from the porch and fisted his fingers as he passed one of the sheds with a lock on the door. The next building was about the size of a single-car garage, with two sliding doors on top hinges that had been pushed open enough in the middle for a person to squeeze through.

When he reached the barn, he thumbed his knuckles against the side of the open wooden door. "Hello?" Houston stepped through the barn door. "Anyone in here?"

Inside, the front section was partitioned out into stalls with a center aisle barely two people wide. A different shaped saddle than he was used to at Natalie's barn. His sister-in-law and her extended family had several horses. This saddle rested on a post of the right stall, and another sat on a cabinet-like bench with brushes and holsters around it. The far side had an open doorway that led to another segment of the barn, or maybe a storage area.

No one answered.

The abnormal noise could have been a rusted door hinge complaining in the wind. Except, the barn's lights were still on. Someone had either fled in a hurry and left some fairly expensive equipment, or he was looking at something worse.

Like someone refusing to evacuate.

Clean straw filled the bottom of the first stall on the left and a plastic bucket filled with fresh water hung on a bent-up nail.

Houston lifted his voice. "I'm Houston James with the Jude County Hotshot crew, and—"

The sound blared again. This time it was no creaking door, but a donkey's cry.

Heavy footsteps thumped toward Houston until the doorway in the middle of the barn was now occupied. Not a donkey, but a mule. He or she stared right at Houston and released another ear-covering shriek.

What was Houston supposed to do with a mule?

"Peanut. Really?" A sing-songy female voice drifted from beyond the mule. "We don't have time for your moods."

A woman came into view and stroked the mule, who Houston assumed was Peanut. "You know that Daisy always loads up first." She petted the mule until her gaze landed on Houston.

"Oh." She wrapped her hand around Peanut's neck as if Houston had planned to steal him. "You're back."

The woman only came up to Houston's shoulders.

Her dark hair was pulled into a ponytail, and a few wisps framed her bright hazel eyes.

Hold on.

He recognized this woman. Didn't he?

Her eyes were both green and brown. A perfect amount of each that used to anchor him back in chemistry class. Houston swallowed and willed words to come. But he couldn't seem to make his tongue work.

The woman had paled and tightened her hold on Peanut. She shook her head. "I'm sorry. I thought you were someone else who had run out of gas earlier."

Houston blinked out of his trance. She didn't recognize him. Maybe this wasn't the girl he knew from high school? "I'm with the Jude County Hotshot Crew. You need to evacuate."

She sighed. "Yes, well, I keep getting interrupted to do just that."

A huge white horse appeared behind her. The beast snorted.

"It's okay, Frank." The woman clicked her tongue. "Time to load up."

The horse, who Houston presumed was Frank, grunted, but made no other movements.

Houston took off his pack. "Here. Let me help. You really shouldn't have left this to the last minute."

She released Peanut and blocked Houston. "I'll take care of them. I am well aware of the importance of loading up my horses."

She avoided his gaze.

Ready or not, the past had hit him again hard in the chest. First with the hesitation to fight the fire and now with his old high school chemistry lab partner. Yes, he knew exactly who this woman was. Or rather, who she'd been years ago. "Rachel, I don't know if you—"

"*Sir*, I understand you're trying to do your job, but your presence isn't going to help my animals load faster. You can get back to the fire. I promise we will leave."

Her eyes snapped to his. Not to any of the burn wounds that reached from the top of his head down his neck, onto his arms and finished their stretch on his side, hidden by his hotshot uniform.

People often stared. Recoiled. Avoided.

What you meant for evil, God meant for good.

But would that even prove true for him?

The woman before Houston treated him almost like his scars weren't there. Like she'd already known about them. "Rachel, let me help. We really have to hurry. Fire isn't anything—"

"I know, Houston." She grabbed Peanut's halter, pulling him back toward Frank in the doorway. Stilled. "Or...whatever you said your name was. But I'm not Rachel."

Her last word was sharp, and Peanut let out another brash bray.

Frank reared back and then sprinted down the stall aisle. Right for Houston.

"Whoa, Frank. Easy. Stop!"

But apparently, the horse wasn't eager to accept his owner's raised voice.

Houston reached out for the animal. But with his ears pressed low and head tucked, Frank was evidently not a horse for a stranger to settle. Houston jumped against the opposite side of the stalls.

"Frank, No!" The woman chased after her white

horse, but Frank galloped away from her and straight out of the barn.

The woman reached the empty doorway, and her chest heaved. She turned and shot a glare Houston didn't think he'd earned. "I told you your presence wouldn't help."

"And I don't think you realize that a fire is coming your way to destroy everything you own, including you."

"Believe me. I know!" She ran back through the doorway in the middle, and Houston followed; however, he did not expect to find her walking a black and white horse out of a rusted horse trailer connected to an equally tarnished truck parked against the barn's rear entrance.

She pulled herself up onto the horse, as if to go after Frank.

"What are you doing?" Houston stepped in front of the horse. "Rachel, you can get fined or even arrested if you don't evacuate—"

"Yes, fine, it's me. And I know, Houston. But I go by Sophie now, and I don't have time to explain that to you. You go do your job. Stop the fire from burning my home. And I promise we'll leave as soon as I find Frank."

Houston extended his arms in front of the barn's exit. "I can't let you risk your life. You're wasting valuable time. The wildfire's—"

"You ignored me once. You can do it again." She spun the horse around and went right through the doorway behind her. "Goodbye, Houston."

Houston clenched his jaw shut. Okay, maybe he deserved that because, yes, he'd failed her. He should have looked her up before now. If only stubbornness wasn't a trait that blossomed during a panic situation. But like she said, there was no time to explain anything.

Houston turned to follow, but at Peanut's most recent bray, he did a double take at the mule, who reached his nose to the stall that held the unusually shaped saddle.

And now the saddle made sense. Mules require a different saddle shape.

Houston was all for saving lives, but he was pretty sure he hadn't signed up for what he was about to ask the mule.

He ran his palm down his face. "You can be ridden, can't you?"

The mule put the hanging stirrups in between his teeth.

Isn't there a better way, Lord? I'm pretty sure I'm going to need a faster beast than Peanut.

But beggars couldn't be picky, especially with a fire coming. And an old friend to save. Houston grabbed the saddle balanced over the top of the side stall in front of him and answered his own question. "Not exactly well, I'd imagine."

His rookie season as a hotshot, and Houston was about to ride a mule to chase after the woman he wanted most to forget.

So much for leaving the past behind.

THREE

THERE WAS NO TIME TO BE WRONG. NOT WHEN HER horse was in danger, and they all had to get out of here.

Sophie clutched the reins in her hands until her fingernails pricked her palms. Even with her eyes watering—from the smoke, not from seeing Houston, thank you very much.

What was the man doing here?

And in a hotshot uniform.

Oh, how the teenage boy from her memories had grown into a man. Even with his scars, he was handsome. Maybe more so. Somehow.

Didn't matter. She'd worry about her Rachel and Sophie worlds colliding later. All she cared about right now was getting Frank and the rest of her horses to safety. Then she'd figure out how to save her ranch.

And then, maybe, she'd ask Houston a few pointed questions. Like *why*?

The breeze carried more ash the deeper she and Daisy moved through the trees. But she couldn't abandon Frank. She would not allow him to feel helpless when she knew all too well what that felt like.

She glanced over her shoulder. Tall pines blocked the view of her ranch. Frank might have circled back and returned to the barn. Her newest horse was smart enough to sense the danger in the air. She couldn't fault him for running.

Her valley hayfield was off to her left, and she eased Daisy up the hill toward the first level of plateaus that surrounded her property. A cough rumbled through her body. Her throat burned, and her chest pulled tight on her next intake of murky air. What if she'd made the wrong choice to come out here? Chasing instead of waiting. All because she was afraid.

Again.

Her legs stiffened in the stirrups. She needed to inhale slowly through her nose. Remain calm. She closed her stinging eyes, and her mind slipped to a memory of another time, long ago, when her lungs had needed more air.

"Mom." Sophie reached for her throbbing ankle.

She pushed something wooden and heavy off and tried to move her foot. Agony shot through her leg. "Dad! Are you guys all right?"

Surely her parents hadn't slept through the earthquake.

Sophie's thunderous heartbeat was the only reply. She hopped toward her darkened doorway but stumbled. Her palm landed on a hard and splintery object.

"Ow!" She pulled her shaking hand toward her face but couldn't see much in the shadows. A trickle of something wet raced down her wrist.

"Rachel." Her father's voice was faint on the other side of the debris wall outside her bedroom door.

She wrapped her palm in the bottom of her pajama shirt and pressed it to her stomach. Tears rolled down her cheeks. "Dad, I'm here. But I—"

"We're...trapped and"—there was a grunt—"can't—"

"My door's blocked. I think the ceiling fell." She wheezed in two quick puffs of air, but it wasn't enough. She pulled the collar of her favorite silk pajamas away from her neck. "Dad, I'm scared."

"Honey," Mom's voice filtered in like a whisper.

"Rachel Sophie, I need you to listen." Dad sounded closer. Had he gotten free? "If you can't get through your door, you'll need to climb out of your window."

Her second-story window, with the porch roof below.

Sophie licked her lips and leaned against what was likely one of the fallen boards from the roof. The pain in her ankle and wrist toyed with a round of dizziness.

Dad mumbled words, and then, "...you have to find help."

Sophie pushed herself up with her left arm. Each hop toward her desk brought tears to her eyes. She opened her blackout curtain, and the sliver of moonlight revealed that the roof had not only collapsed in front of her door, but a tree limb poked through the top of the windowpane. The only way to exit her window was through the half-broken section at the bottom.

"Dad, I can't do it!" More tears rolled down her face. If only her brother were at home.

She wasn't the answer. Help would have to come to them.

Sophie blinked at the trees swaying in front of her. The bend of the saddle beneath her. She was outside, not in her bedroom. Not trapped. No longer helpless.

She tightened her legs around Daisy. With a deep inhale, she put her hand to her mouth again and whistled. She scanned the hazy field below them in the valley and then, as she swung her gaze up the hillside, Daisy's ears twisted.

"You hear him, girl?"

Leaves crunched. Then once more. It came from behind. Sophie steered Daisy back toward the barn, only to pull up on the reins. Houston.

And he was on…Peanut?

If Frank wasn't lost, and wildfire wasn't coming to destroy all the things she loved, seeing Houston bend his legs up in the stirrups so as not to drag along the ground would be humorous. And maybe a little bit like revenge.

Instead, Sophie shook her head. He should be doing his job by trying to stop the fire. Out here on Peanut, he wasted both of their time by trying to stop her from saving Frank.

She turned Daisy. "I'm not coming back until—"

"Let's find Frank." He didn't stop Peanut as they neared. He simply shifted the reins in his hands, far better than Jonah had done this morning, and directed Peanut to climb up the incline deeper into the forest. "I'll get on top and look down on the other side."

That actually was a good plan. Except…"Frank doesn't know you. He'll get even more spooked. Which is why he ran in the first place."

Houston sent her a look as if that was a given. Then he and Peanut climbed to the flat plateau section out of her viewpoint.

She clicked her tongue to go straight through the young pines growing in the shadows of the mature trees. The murky smoke resting in the low branches blocked the treetops.

"I don't see him, do you?"

She squinted out over the valley and inspected the trees on the opposite side. Had Frank gone over there? Usually, he ran toward his right. "No. Let's try down in that valley. There's an apple tree there he likes to search for dropped fruit." The horse was ever hopeful, even out of harvest season.

She nudged her horse down a rocky path.

"I'll take the higher route above as you lead." Houston directed Peanut upward with a little grunt. Then his soft tone drifted to her. "How long have you lived here?"

Was he for real? After what he did to her in high school, did he really think she wanted to be all chummy now?

"Houston." It was easier to express herself when she couldn't see his face. And it had nothing to do with his scars. "There's no time to chitchat. We aren't friends. You made that clear before. I have to find Frank. And like it or not, I don't have to explain anything else to you."

After a beat, he said, "I was trying to get you talking so Frank might hear you and feel safe enough to come your way."

"Oh." Was all she could manage.

"And I assumed he could tell whether your tone is calm or not. Horses are smart."

Horses weren't the only smart thing around. Houston may have once been her reluctant, borderline delinquent chemistry class lab partner—one she once thought was her friend—but he could never be classified as dumb. "That's...a good idea, actually."

Seeing him here, in a fireman's jacket, might be the last thing she expected. Clearly this was her day for the past to haunt her. But just because he'd walked back into her life didn't mean she needed to let him in.

Sophie steered Daisy around a hole in the dirt up ahead and refused to think about Frank possibly stepping in such a hole and getting hurt. "Frank! Come on, bud."

Only the steps of Daisy and Peanut's feet stomping over the leaves and fallen sticks filled the silence. Normally, she loved the sound of peace. The stillness quieted her fears, but right in this moment, she felt anything but that comfort.

Sophie traced her thumb over the worn leather on Daisy's reins. They were running out of time, but perhaps Houston's plan could work.

After a few moments of quiet scanning, Sophie pressed her lips together. "Umm, how long have you been on the hotshot team...or crew?" That was the last job she pictured him wanting after what happened to him. "I'm not sure what they're called."

Daisy took five more steps.

Still no answer from her previously unwanted partner. Only what resembled a humming noise. Another blast of smoke filled her nose. The path in front of her narrowing from the amount of smoke staking its new claim. Not good. The fire was moving toward them, creeping through the brush like a stalking predator.

Her throat constricted. "Houston?"

"I see him," came his hushed reply. He edged into view and nodded his chin over the rise of the plateau where she couldn't see. "I'm going to try and push Frank down toward you."

"Wait," Sophie hissed between two coughs.

Houston and Peanut disappeared into the smoke.

Frank should see *her* first before Houston's presence here surprised him. The last thing they needed was a galloping chase through uneven, root-filled ground. Farther away from escape.

She could *not* deal with another horse's death.

She'd already lost enough.

Her chest squeezed. She wasn't sure if it was the air quality, the situation, or both. Before Sophie could manage a decision, Frank's face popped into view over the hill. Peanut's head came right beside her previously rogue horse.

Sophie sent Daisy climbing up the incline. "I can't believe…"

Houston was not on Peanut. He was actually sitting on Frank. Without a saddle.

Sophie's mouth gaped open.

Obviously, she knew little about this version of Houston, the hotshot firefighter.

He wasn't the selfish teen boy she'd known.

"How did you…" *Get Frank to trust you. Switch from Peanut to Frank. Learn to ride so well. Arrive in Ember.*

All of those questions begged to find answers, but none escaped her mouth.

"Let's get back." Houston held Frank's reins in one hand and petted her runaway horse's neck with the other.

Most women thought a man in uniform was a sight to behold. But for Sophie, there was something about a man on a horse who understood what he was doing that she couldn't look away from.

Not fair. He'd stood her up without a backward glance. But one moment back in her life, and she couldn't take her eyes off him.

Nope. She didn't know why fate—or God—had

brought him back into her life. She wasn't biting. This time, she'd be the one who didn't look back.

She blinked. "Right. Yes. I've got to get everyone loaded, but I think you should ride Daisy, and I'll ride Frank. Just in case he tries to pull anything again."

She forced her shoulders back, ready for a fight. Houston's posture proved he'd ridden more than she expected, however she couldn't chance Frank freaking out again.

Houston lifted his eyebrow, the one that wasn't scarred, but then nodded.

Sophie slipped off Daisy and grabbed onto all three of her animals. "How did you get Frank to come up to you?"

Houston gave her his crooked grin that once made her stomach flutter. "It was more Peanut than me. That and I...prayed."

Prayer. Right. Something she should have been doing this entire time.

"I hummed an old hymn. Frank came nose to nose with Peanut, and I grabbed his leads." Houston dismounted right in front of her. Only a few inches remained between them. His eyes were a deeper brown coloring than both Pudding and Chestnut's fur, with a dusting of gold flaked throughout.

"Thank you." Aw, her voice came out all breathless. Like he still had an effect on her.

He leaned closer. The smell of smoke disappeared for a moment, and in its place, hints of cinnamon and honey hung in the air. She had never smelled such a combination on a man before.

Unfortunately, she didn't hate it.

Houston lowered his head. "Sorry for spooking Frank. And for what happened that night —"

"You're right. We've got to get out of here. Thanks again for helping find Frank." She pulled herself up onto the wayward horse. "You have no idea what it would have been like...to lose something else I love."

Houston looked away. "I think everyone can relate to losing things."

He climbed up on Daisy and headed down the slope toward the field, giving Sophie nowhere else to look except the back of his head. Right at Houston's burn scars.

Of course, Houston understood what it was like to suffer loss.

Up ahead, he steered Daisy to the left of a hole in the dirt. As Sophie took Frank and Peanut nearer the pile of dirt, Frank's ears twisted back, and Peanut stopped walking.

"What is it, guys?" As they rounded the dirt pile, Sophie gasped.

Houston spun around. "You okay?"

There was no time to understand why her pulse fluttered at the compassion in Houston's voice. Her finger shook as she pointed at what stuck halfway out of the dirt pile.

Two very charred human feet.

Sophie blinked. "There's a body in the dirt."

Apparently, today was that day. The kind of day where one problem found the next. And he was the collector.

"What do we do?" Sophie voiced Houston's thoughts.

The fire roaring their way was trouble enough,

but the good news of finding Frank had been extinguished. And, for a second, they'd actually been working as a team. He'd thought that maybe God had engineered this crazy meet up to give him another chance. To apologize, and maybe make things right with Rachel. If he hadn't stood her up, his entire past might have been different.

But for now, they had a dead body to deal with.

He went to pull his phone out of his cargo pocket, until he remembered he left it charging in his locker. "Do you have a phone? First, we'll call 911."

"There's no point." Sophie had paled as her gaze remained on the charred feet poking out of the dirt. "There's no signal out here. Only closer to the barn."

"That's okay, I have something better." He grabbed for his radio. But it wasn't in his other pocket. It had either dropped out, or it was in his pack. The pack he shouldn't have left at the barn.

Now, they had no way of contacting anyone.

"What do you think happened?" Sophie whispered.

Houston turned Daisy in a circle. The trees stood watch but gave no hint as to what they might have witnessed. Whether accident or murder. "There aren't any footprints or tire tracks."

Sophie's question still hung in the thick and hazy air. And that's when he heard it, the thing he'd somehow forgotten. Not the branches creaking in the breeze, but the sizzle of sap in the distance burning in flames. Dead body or not, the fire wasn't stopping. There's no way the police would arrive here before the fire. Which meant that anything left in the crime scene would be obliterated—including the body. Better to salvage *something*.

"We've got to get out here. Now." He pointed to the mound of dirt. "And we've got to take the body with us." He jumped off of Daisy and looped the reins around a tree branch.

"Houston, we can't. The sheriff has to—"

"Rach…I mean, Sophie." Houston's voice was softer than his boots on the leaves on the ground. Why had she changed her name? There was plenty about this woman he'd missed since they last saw each other. And part of him wanted to learn it all.

Except there was no time.

"If you have your phone, take a few quick pictures and video of the area. I'm going to put the body on Peanut." The mule would have no problem carrying the weight. "If we don't evacuate with the body, the police may never identify the person, let alone what happened."

"I hate that you're right." Sophie held up her phone. "No offense."

Right or not, there wasn't even time for a plan. Instead, Houston dropped to his knees. He had to get the body uncovered. As he pushed the dirt away, his watch scratched along a blue tarp.

A cough from Sophie quickened Houston's movements. The air grew thicker. Grayer. More troubled. They didn't have a minute to waste, and if a tarp was wrapped around the body, Houston wouldn't contaminate anything with his hands.

He shoved off the dirt. However, when his palm knocked dirt away, part of the tarp unwrapped, revealing half of the body's scorched face.

The man's eyes were missing but his teeth were there, and his skin had been singed.

Houston's eyes squeezed shut, but darkness didn't

erase the flashback to when he was eighteen and was awakened in an ambulance by screams. *His* screams. There had been so many flames. Smoke. And the searing pain. All from the house fire he had accidentally helped start.

Houston's hands went to the back of his bald head, where his hair no longer grew because of his scars. The pain was over, but the consequences of his actions remained.

He knew exactly what this man had been through.

"Houston." Sophie's voice and hand on his shoulder anchored him in the present. "You don't have to do this alone. I'll help lift."

Houston exhaled. The tautness in his chest eased. "It's going to be heavy."

She squatted beside him. "The things that are worth doing usually are, aren't they? I've pulled Peanut right behind us. You ready?"

Houston stared at her for a second before he nodded. "Together. On three. One…two…"

Sophie groaned out, "Three."

A coppery, sour odor reached his nose.

"Just one step at a time." Houston adjusted more of the weight toward his side.

They took two more steps. He dug his fingers into the slick plastic, except the bottom of the tarp was wet. From blood or moisture from the ground. Probably both.

Despite his recent past, Houston still believed God didn't create accidents or coincidences. But surely there was someone far better qualified to find a dead body. One of the guys on the crew used to be a cop, didn't he? He was pretty sure Dakota had mentioned being a SWAT officer. Then again, there was never a great day to find someone dead. And Houston had been the one to volunteer for this evacuation mission.

Houston shifted the body higher. They were almost to Peanut. But then a gust of air thrust against his back, a cloud of dark smoke circled around them, and the tarp flapped open, revealing more than they ever wanted to see.

Another cough jarred Sophie, and her end of the body sagged. "I-I can't."

Houston arched his back, took the extra weight, and heaved the body over Peanut's back.

Sophie bent over. Her hands on her knees. "I'm sorry, Houston. I…"

He rested his hand on her shoulder. "I promise you just being here helped." He squeezed his fingers, then released her.

The pop of the flames grew louder. He didn't know how close the fire had reached on the other side of the plateau, but no matter where it was, they had to leave. Now.

After unlooping Daisy's reins, he climbed up on the saddle while Sophie pulled herself onto Frank and hung on to Peanut's leads.

Traveling back to the barn, they kept a steady pace. At least he prayed they were heading in the right direction. The air resembled a blizzard, only grayer, and pieces of ash collected in Sophie's ponytail.

Houston stayed as near to Peanut as possible in case the body might slip off. Finally, the peak of the barn roof came into view. "Do you have a signal yet?"

Sophie passed him Peanut's leads and pulled out her phone. "I'll try the sheriff's office directly." She pushed a couple of buttons, and then the phone rang over her speaker.

A man answered. "Hello, Ember Sheriff."

"Sherrif, it's Sophie Lamb." She glanced at Houston. Then the body. "Sir, I don't know how to tell you this, but we've found a dead body at the ranch. The fire's coming, and we had to move it."

Jumping in was one way to tell it how it was.

"I'm sorry." The Sherrif's voice pitched higher. "One more time."

She moved her phone out toward Houston.

"Sir. This is Houston James. I'm with the Jude County Hotshots. Sophie and I moved a dead body due to evacuation orders and—"

"Dead body. I was afraid that's what you said." The man mumbled something that Houston couldn't understand. Then he said, "I can't spare any of my guys to send your way. Even if I could, if you're in the fire's line, we won't get to you in time. But most importantly, get out. And second, can you get the body here safely?"

"Yes, sir." Sophie nodded. "We'll get into town as soon as we can."

"Then I'll see you when you get here. Be careful. We've already dealt with too many incidents today."

Sophie pocketed her phone and steered them toward the back of the barn. "I'll load up Frank and Daisy first."

Houston kept his attention on the deep gray smoke swirling above the treetops. The corner of the barn's siding flapped in the wind that was picking up speed. Which meant the fire could reach them even sooner. "I'll unload the body in the back of your truck bed. Then Peanut."

And his pack. He never should have left it. A rookie mistake. Hopefully, he could find his radio if it had dropped out of his pocket.

They made it past the pasture gate and around to her parked truck and horse trailer. Everything went as planned for once today. Houston slid the body off Peanut and closed the tailgate. As Sophie loaded Peanut in behind Frank and Daisy, Houston ran for his pack inside the barn, and there by the stall that had held Peanut's saddle was where his radio rested in the straw.

With gear on, he met Sophie at the horse trailer as she shut the ramp. "Let's get you out of here." There would not be any more chasing things. "Are you driving, or am I?"

She headed to the driver's side. "Of course I'm driving. It's my truck."

He hopped in the other side, and she pulled away from the barn.

"I've got to radio my boss." Houston fished out his radio and reached out a call to update his chief. He didn't answer. Probably too busy fighting the flames. Houston rerouted his call and radioed HQ.

"Sounds like you're exactly where you need to be," Commander Dafoe's tone rang with confidence. "Stay safe, James. Over and out."

Exactly where he needed to be? Houston tapped his fist against the truck's dash. He was supposed to be fighting fires, not running into Sophie and finding a body.

But right now, he had a task to complete. Get her to safety. Get the body to the sheriff. Then he could get back to what he was hired to do. Battle fires.

"You all right?" Sophie asked with her eyes on the road.

Houston shifted in the passenger seat. "Fine. Do you have somewhere safe to ride out the fire? If not, there's temporary shelter at the high school. Hopefully, my crew will have the fire under control soon and you can come home."

She glanced at him then, her eyes big and beautiful. Hazel was definitely an underrated color. But strangely, they weren't filled with irritation or disgust as he probably deserved for their high school past.

"You don't have to keep worrying about me, Houston. After we take the body to the sheriff's, I'll be out of your hair."

And maybe that was the other problem. He was running out of time. Perhaps God had provided this reunion for a reason. God had given him a second chance at life when He'd saved Houston from the fire. He didn't want to mess up this chance between him and Sophie. And based on the tightness in his stomach, Houston knew exactly what he should do with the quiet cab time.

But instead, his mouth had its own plan. "Had you always hoped to leave Last Chance County?"

"Not exactly." She shrugged. "Short story is I inherited this ranch."

One of the truck tires hit a pothole on the road, and Houston steadied his hand against the passenger door. "That actually makes sense of why you have the horses."

She whipped her gaze his way. "They weren't inherited. I rescued them."

Houston studied the inner green of her eyes that

matched the trees blurring past his passenger side window. The slight raise of her tone made him well aware that there was definitely a longer version of her story. And he wanted to hear it.

He loosened his seatbelt across his chest. "They are lucky to have you."

Sophie turned the radio down. "What about you? How did you end up here in Ember?"

Houston glanced out the window. What he could see of the trees, their tops were not only bending but their middles were swaying too. The wind needed to stop.

"Recently, I guess I wanted to become a hotshot to understand more of what my brother goes through. Macon's a firefighter. And it seemed like a good plan to help me save enough money for my upcoming seminary schooling."

She kept her gaze on the road. "Firefighter and seminary. Guess we've both changed a lot since high school."

Pride tasted sour as he swallowed. "I was a self-focused idiot back in high school, Rach—Sophie. I need to explain what happened. And I'm sorry for—"

"Really, Houston." She held up her palm. "Please, leave the past alone."

Her knuckles tightened around the leather steering wheel. A crease formed along her forehead. One he'd caused. No, the easier option was to leave the past alone. Didn't make it the right one.

He turned toward her. "I was shocked to find your letter in my locker wanting to meet me that night."

Sophie grunted. "So shocked that you didn't know how to let me down gently, so instead you sent your brother in your place. If you meant for him to ease the blow of your rejection, it didn't work like that. Then to be denied visiting you at the hospital." She slashed her hand through the air. "The past doesn't matter. I'm more concerned about saving what I have *now*. I can't lose my ranch." Her mouth formed a thin line and then she mumbled, "And I have to make sure I'm not going crazy."

The city limits sign came into view, and Houston peeked over at Sophie. "I'm also sorry I had the nurse prevent you from visiting." When he'd first awakened from sedation in the hospital, the pain from his burns had been too much for him to be able to focus on any conversation. Not that he should have ignored her after sending his brother in his place for what she must have thought would have been a date. And it wasn't like Houston had not wanted to date her, it was that he shouldn't have.

He rubbed his thumb along his forehead. She didn't want to deal with the past. But he could at least help her with her future. "Turns out, I'm a good listener. Not as good as you always were, but—"

Sophie slammed on the brakes and stared at the red stoplight as Houston stole glances at her. A variety of vehicles were parked along Ember's downtown, and people bustled about as if a forest fire wasn't knocking on the town's door. Even though the arrows posted on the street posts for the temporary shelter at the high school were as real as the nightmare in the back of the truck bed.

As if she heard his thoughts, her gaze drifted to the rearview mirror. "This day has been...first Thunderbolt. Then I-I thought I saw my brother today, but they say that can't be. And now you and the dead body."

At the tremor in her voice, he reached for her, but then fisted his fingers. He remembered she had an older brother. One that served as her guardian after her parents' deaths, but Houston had never met him. "Why can't you see your brother?"

Sophie pulled up to the curb in front of the police department and put the truck in Park. The silence in the cab heated hotter than the fire Orion had stomped out in the woods.

She unbuckled her seatbelt. "Three years ago today, Homeland Security told me that he'd died. But with no body to bury..." She combed her shaking fingers through her ponytail. "Looks like you've gotten your act together since high school, and I'm the one left being a stubborn fool."

At that, she hopped out of the truck and slammed the door.

Teenage Sophie had had a golden heart. The quiet girl who convinced him that being her chemistry lab partner would make science more fun. She'd been right. And now, her heart was breaking not only due to the fear of losing her ranch, but also from losing her brother.

Houston may not be able to make the past up to her, but he would do everything in his power to save her ranch.

FOUR

THERE WAS A LOT SOPHIE COULDN'T CONTROL about the day. But she refused to dig through some of her most embarrassing high school memories. That and she couldn't let anyone connect any dots that might lead to more questions about her brother. To her knowledge, Houston had never met Crispin. Yet once again, she'd found him easy to talk to. Why him of all people?

She marched around her truck. Seven parking meters begging for payment reminded her she had exactly ninety-two dollars on her. Sixty that stayed in the truck and thirty-two in her purse. She should have made time to grab her safe or at least her old family photobook from her house. And she hated the thought of her grandma's sewing machine surviving an earthquake but not a fire.

Her eyes burned. This time not from the air quality. As long as her horses were safe, she could rebuild everything else. That was, if she had enough insurance coverage.

When she stepped closer to the meter, she

stumbled. She reached out for the closest meter, but it was Houston who caught her.

"Okay there?" His breath tickled against her neck as he inspected her with a frown.

"Sophie Lamb, is that you in the flesh?" Betty Adams had her usual shoulder length hair cut into a shorter bob, and her peppered gray hair was now a polished black color. Her husband, Robert, was right beside her and looked the exact same as usual—spray-tanned and wearing an outfit color-coordinated with his wife. Today his salmon-colored polo matched the flowers on Betty's blouse.

"We were so worried about you." Betty let go of Robert's arm as he held tight to the three boutique bags he had in his grip.

Robert bobbed his dimpled chin. "We'd heard the fire had the old Valley Ranch in its sights."

Betty tsked. "It's Sophie's place now." She placed her hand toward Houston. "We're the Adams."

"Houston James, Jude County hotshot."

"Yes, I see that." Her gaze bounced between Houston and Sophie as if waiting for more. "My husband, Robert, and I went to school with the previous owner's family. Though I assumed the Whites would have claimed the ranch as theirs. Their loss is Sophie's gain, I suppose." Her penciled eyebrows lowered. "Though I will say, it's still a bit confusing how you inherited the place. I haven't heard the entire story."

Neither had Sophie. She wasn't entirely sure how Crispin had arranged for her to get her dream property either. But it could have only been him. There were no other possible connections. "I'm afraid we really need to go talk to the sheriff right now."

"That family claims everything else in this town. It's time for new blood," Robert grumbled, completely ignoring what she said.

Houston shifted. "It was nice to meet you, but—"

"They can't claim me, hun, I'm all yours." Betty patted Robert's rounded stomach and then turned back to Sophie. "Have you had a chance to rename Valley Ranch, or are you keeping it the same for the time being? Little Lamb Ranch does have a nice ring to it, wouldn't you say so?"

"I'll have to get back to you on that. We have an appointment..." Sophie pointed to the police station and took a step, but Betty walked toward the horse trailer.

She stretched her hand out toward the window Frank just pulled his head away from. Sophie sent a glance to Houston. "Maybe it's better if I stay out here, and you—"

"I've also heard that your horses might be in the new movie." Betty batted her lashes. "How exciting. If only I were younger. Right, hun? I'd be a marvelous movie actress."

Robert nodded with a grin.

"To be in a movie would just be..." She rested her elbow on the back ledge of Sophie's truck. "Perhaps...you could talk to the director for me? It would be a dream to meet Winchester Marshall."

The sheriff's car pulled in front of Sophie's truck. Finally.

Sophie grimaced. "I really don't have any authority on set."

The wind picked up and sent Sophie's ponytail dancing. As Houston spun around, his eyes set on the horizon, Betty's gaze dipped to the flapping tarp in the back of the truck. The body peeked out of the tarp, and Betty shrieked.

The sheriff jumped out of his car. His hair only had a few stripes of gray, but he wore wisdom in the crinkles around his eyes. Sheriff was listed over his name tag that said Hutchinson.

He took one look at Sophie and Houston, then to screaming Betty. "Betty!"

She closed her red painted mouth, but her bottom lip trembled. "Is that a body? What on earth has happened?"

A man older than all of them pushed his walker their way on the sidewalk. "What needs to happen is for someone to move that there trailer." He aimed his bony finger at Sophie's horse trailer. "You're taking up my parking spot."

Betty shook her head as she centered one of the rings on her finger. "Gerald, there's no time for that. Someone's died, and we're about to learn how and why."

The sheriff crossed his arms. "No one is going to be finding anything out here on the sidewalk. It's time to be on your way."

Gerald rose on his scuffed white tennis shoes. His walker tipped forward a bit too far. "I don't see a dead horse back here."

"Gerald Eugene. Hush!" Betty fluttered her wrist at the man. "We're not talking about a dead horse, but a dead person."

Four other people had now gathered at the front of Sophie's truck. Great. More gossip.

A young woman with her hair pulled into a braid snuggled her infant baby closer to her chest. Beside her was a suited William, the bank loan representative. Of course, he'd be the one to see. Hopefully, this wouldn't reflect on her application.

The young woman spun around with her baby and almost hit a lanky teen who shoved through the crowd. When the boy looked up, a familiar gaze locked onto Sophie and turned stormy.

"Lewis."

Houston's shoulder brushed past Sophie as he stepped toward Lewis. "Hey, you."

The teen's eyes bugged at Houston. He dropped his skateboard onto the sidewalk and flew past Gerald, clipping the older man's shoulder.

Gerald gripped his walker. "You all are witnesses. He keeps trying to knock me over. Arrest that delinquent. You saw him this time, Sheriff!"

The sheriff turned to Houston. "I assume you had a run in with Lewis too?"

Sophie leaned against her trailer. Poor Marley, what had her nephew done now? Her friend would be devastated.

Houston said, "We found him and two others, ignoring evacuations and setting off firecrackers near the fire."

"Probably Finn and Preston. Those two are trouble." The sheriff sighed. "If Lewis could stay clear of them, he might have a chance to get off my radar."

Sophie dipped her head. "I tried to help him by giving him a job, but I had to let him go. Being late I could overlook, but stealing..." Especially without repentance.

"You should have filed a report on that. Let's hope none of those young men had anything to do with the reason you called." The sheriff gestured toward the front of Sophie's truck. "It's time for everyone to move along."

She wanted to go after Lewis, but the teen had already disappeared behind a building.

"I am moving along." Gerald shuffled past. "Moving farther along than I wanted because of how she parked that there truck." His neck wobbled as he shook his head. "Back in my day, elders were given respect."

"I'll be by when I can, Gerald. I'll help you unload the dog food from your truck." The sheriff spoke to Gerald but stared down Betty and Robert.

Betty's heels clicked against the pavement. Closer. Not further away, as directed. "Sophie dearest, if you found that body..." She pressed her hand to her chest. "I can't imagine what you've been through. If you need anything, or someone to talk to, I'm only a call away. You have my number, right?"

As if Sophie wanted to give her more fodder for gossip. *I'm not the one who screamed when I saw the body.*

"Thanks, Betty." The sheriff sent a glare toward her husband. "I'll take it from here."

Robert jostled the bags on his arms and steered his wife away. "Come on, darlin', let's go get you one of your favorite coffees."

Once everyone was gone except Houston and Sophie, the sheriff walked over to the truck and lifted a section of the tarp. A brief grimace showed before he masked his expression.

He twisted his mouth to the side. "I'm afraid the entire town will know too much all too soon. Especially if Robert's taking her to the coffee shop. Wish I could have gotten here quicker." He glanced at Houston. "Could you help me unload the body on the gurney and wheel it down to the coroner? All my other officers are out right now. The fire's not the only thing hitting the town hard. Burglaries. A wreck. And an assault. It's been a mess."

Houston's gaze first went to Sophie, filled with something she couldn't quite read. "Of course."

"Sophie!" Marley's voice had Sophie searching for her friend.

Marley waved from the road from the driver's seat of her white van with flowers painted on the sides, along with the name of the florist shop she helped run.

The sheriff gave his chin a nod. "You might as well warn Marley for me that I'll be by her house sometime to ask Lewis some questions."

"Will do," Sophie said over her shoulder as she hurried across the road.

Marley's curls had been pulled into a knot on her head, but pieces of hair had come loose around her neck. Sophie couldn't miss the dark shadows under Marley's eyes.

Marley twisted the ring on her thumb. "Please tell me you've seen Lewis."

Sophie pointed behind her. "He flew past on his skateboard. But I'm afraid he's long gone."

Marley leaned her head back in the seat. "It's official. He hates me."

"He doesn't hate you." Though he did more than likely hate Sophie, since she fired him.

A car honked behind Marley, and Sophie waved the red car around.

Marley's knuckles were white as she gripped her fuzzy steering wheel cover. "Maybe I shouldn't have taken away his cell phone *and* his beloved four-wheeler for stealing your money? Maybe then I could reach him about the evacuation."

Houston's words about Lewis in the woods had Sophie saying, "Something tells me he knows about the evacuation already."

Marley's face blanched. "Why? What has he done now?"

"The sheriff said he'd be by later to chat. I would help you look, but..." Sophie stuck her head closer inside the window. "We found a dead body at the ranch. That's why I'm here instead of taking the horses straight to the set's livery. We had to bring the body to the sheriff because of the fire."

Marley blinked her blue eyes at her. Twice. "Like...a real..."

Sophie shuddered. "Yes."

"Girl, are you okay? I can't even..." Marley's eyebrows shot up. "We as in *Lewis*? Did he have anything to do...you said he ran off?"

"No, a hotshot firefighter who came to the house to make sure I'd evacuated helped me."

Marley pressed her hands to her chest. "At least that's good. Why did I ever tell my brother that watching Lewis for a year during his deployment would be super easy? What I need is a full body massage, and what do you say about moving to the beach? They need horse whisperers down there too, right? Please say you'll move with me. Let's just start over."

She nearly laughed at that offer but glanced over her shoulder at where Houston had been standing. "I'm sure starting over won't erase all your problems."

Or the past.

"I've got to see if Houston needs help and then get

my horses away from the fire. Rain check? Oh, how did the flower delivery go to Kathryn? Or did you chicken out and only talk to her assistant?"

"Stupid fire," Marley mumbled. "I managed an 'I adore your movies' to her before my mouth stopped working, and her assistant took the bouquet. Kathryn did say that the flowers were the yellowest roses she'd ever seen." Then Marley narrowed her eyes. "But don't think you can change the subject. Who's Houston?"

Sophie's cheeks should not be heating right now. She dusted off Marley's van window seal. "The hotshot firefighter. Remember? He helped get my horses loaded and with the other thing."

Sophie didn't need to look at her friend to know she was inspecting her. The woman had a knack for reading Sophie's mind, even from the first day they met at Marley's horse-riding lessons. "Right. Sure. So, I'm gonna need a rain check for that entire story with the cute hotshot firefighter."

"There's not much to tell."

Marley gave her a wide grin. "So, he is cute."

Sophie rolled her eyes as Marley cupped her hands under her chin.

Another car honked behind Marley. "Better go. Call me immediately if you see Lewis again. And don't ignore my call later. I deserve to be on the listening side of a juicy story for once. I'm tired of Betty making up stuff about us selling the wrong kind of tulips. Hey, let's do dinner at my house at six. I'll make fajitas."

"Sounds good. But you're going to be disappointed. There isn't much of a story to tell." Or at least that's what Sophie kept telling herself. The knot in her stomach seemed to have a different viewpoint.

As Sophie walked back toward her truck, her phone dinged. Due to smoke from the fire, the director was no longer reshooting the last scene. Sophie was free to come get her horses at her convenience.

She paused on the steps of the station and returned a text to Cosmos asking if she could leave all of her horses in the set's barn for a bit longer. Hopefully, after the fire had been extinguished, she'd still have a ranch to go home to.

She pulled open the door to the police station just as the sheriff ran past, flipped on his car siren, and pulled away. Sophie prayed that wasn't a foreshadowing of the rest of her day.

"Do you want the good news or the bad?" Houston said as he met up with Sophie by the police station's door. The front receptionist had her ear pressed to the phone and her attention locked on her computer.

Sophie slipped her own cell into her back jeans pocket. "Some good would be great right about now."

The half smile made him wish he had better news. "You can go back home."

Her smile grew until it made her beautiful eyes light up. She started toward him as if to what, hug him?

His pulse pounded in his temples.

But instead, she rocked backward and crossed her arms over her chest. "The fire's gone, then?"

He cleared his throat and pointed to the doorway.

"Not exactly. I've just got off with my commander. The wind has changed direction. Which means you can return home to grab your important stuff that we didn't have time for earlier. It's a tentative return, not official."

Not yet. He didn't want to get her hopes up.

She raised her chin. "And the bad?"

Houston shrugged. "You're stuck with me for a while longer."

She pushed her ponytail over her shoulder. "Oh."

Was that a good or bad response? Or maybe both? "I have to assess at ground level. See if the mandatory evacuation is still needed." And to oversee her departure if she couldn't stay.

A crease formed across her forehead. "Can we go now? I don't want to keep the horses cooped up longer than necessary. Or do I need to give a statement about the body?"

"On his way out to another emergency, the sheriff said for you to text him the pictures you took on your phone, and he'd get in contact with us as soon as he could. Hopefully, the fire didn't touch the gravesite at your ranch. He also mentioned it would take the coroner a while to figure out details about the body."

Back in the truck, silence remained until they hit the "Come Back to Ember" sign. "So…" Her voice was hesitant as she moved her hands to ten and two on the wheel. "Was it hard training to be a hotshot firefighter with your obvious experience with fire? Facing your fears, I guess is what I'm asking. And… it's okay if you don't want to answer. I did say we had enough problems in the present to not…well, you know. But technically, you becoming a firefighter has to do with the here and now. Plus, you probably get asked that a lot."

Houston pulled his collar away from the scars on his neck. "Rarely actually."

"Really?"

"I mean, my brother Macon questions my sanity. And his wife Natalie still wants to pull me in for counseling. She's a therapist—and whose family I learned riding from. But no, most of the time, people, once they get over the shock of how I look, they sidestep my scars." Sidestep him. "Well, adults more than kids."

"Do Macon and his wife have kids?"

"Not yet. The kids I meant were my old youth group." They'd seen the real him, not what his body looked like.

"I bet you were good with them, the kids." Her voice lowered to match the hum of the truck engine.

"Thought I was." Houston repositioned his pack nestled in the floorboard between his legs. "The fire provided me a second chance at life, and I wanted to share how God had redeemed me. Doors opened, and I became the youth pastor at Last Chance County Church."

She frowned. "What happened that made you come here instead? I don't think it's only because you wanted to know how your brother's job worked."

Sophie always had been too observant. Houston crossed his arms. Smoke drifted above the tops of the branches out the front windshield. Not exactly the good sign they needed for Sophie to fully return home.

Sophie drummed her fingers on top of the steering wheel. "You don't have to tell me if you don't want. I know what it's like to have God veer you from your plan."

Your plan. As in Houston's plan. Not God's.

Was that what he'd been doing?

Houston sighed. "I tried to help one of the families of my youth group kids. While I was at their house, the mother…well…later she lied and said I came onto her. She was very vocal about my accused actions, and the elders wanted to avoid a scandal. But I'm pretty sure they had been searching for a way to give my job to the pastor's newly graduated son."

"Sorry, Houston." Sophie checked her rearview mirror. "That sucks."

It did. Houston leaned his shoulders back. "But God has provided a temporary job for me to help save for seminary. Then I'm sure He'll provide a new church job." Until Houston got to help people spiritually again, he'd make sure they were safe physically.

The road curved out of town, and the treetops were no longer swaying. No burned sections were visible from the road. The crew's dug fire line had held.

In the valley below, Sophie's ranch came into view. And the leaves and ground remained a comforting green coloring.

"It's still there," Sophie whispered.

As they passed under a welded arched sign that read, *Valley Ranch*, Houston leaned forward in his seat. Now it was up to him whether or not she could stay.

She pulled the truck to a stop in front of her house and turned off the engine. The pillows resting against the wooden porch swing gave a come and sit allure, but the sudden bending of the treetops lining the valley made his stomach tighten.

Wind plus the smallest spark could produce an entire sea of flames. *What if the firebreak doesn't hold?*

Houston unbuckled first. "I'm going to check for any damage."

She hopped out of the truck. "I'm going to release the horses."

Houston pivoted. "Let's wait on that."

The last thing he wanted to do was chase after Frank while riding Peanut for a second time today.

"If that's your way of saying we're not staying and I need to go dig out my safe from under the bed, message received." Her shoulders hunched as she headed for her porch.

He closed the truck's side door. "I'm not sure of anything yet." The haze in the air hadn't cleared up much since they'd left. The wind blew at his back, which was a little too much déjà vu. He stared at the tallest pines in view along the plateau on the barn's side of the property.

The fire had changed directions. Hadn't it?

He paused by the bottom of her porch and watched the branches sway and bend toward the house. The exact same way they had when he'd knocked the last time.

"Oh, no!"

Houston spun around, too slow to catch the rectangular black object. Her phone hit the concrete step beside his boot. He picked it up. "I think it's okay. Nothing's cracked."

"Finally, something's gone right." When she lifted her head and smiled, he realized too late he should have already stepped back.

They were too close.

With her face right below his, he could count every faint freckle along her hairline. She had three on the right and two darker ones on the left. There was even one faded freckle beside her nose.

Houston swallowed. She had been pretty in high school, and still was, but she was so much more than her appearance.

It was probably a good thing he'd known about his brother's crush, or Houston might have tried to date her back in school. That would have been disastrous for her, given the path he'd been on back then. Before the fire changed more than his appearance. God had showed him His gift of redemption.

A piece of hair flew in front of her face and dangled in her eyelashes.

Houston tucked it back behind her ear. His thumb brushed against her cheek, and she shivered. He lowered his hands as if to rub them along the goosebumps on her arms. "I really need to tell you why I sent Macon that day..."

But she stepped back and ran up the steps.

She opened her front door, her cheeks flushed. "If you don't think I can stay, I'll get my safe while you..."

She stood gaping into her house. At her gasp, Houston took the steps two at a time.

Glass shards shimmered along the hardwood. Her cabinet doors were open. Books and bills and placemats and bowls all scattered.

Someone had looted her house.

Not unheard of during an evacuation. The sheriff had mentioned burglaries today, but that didn't make it easier to deal with. Houston stepped in front of her.

The person could still be here.

She pointed at the television hanging on the wallpapered wall. "They took a picture."

He squinted at what could be an empty nail beside the television. A picture was what she noticed in the mess? "The photo could have fallen in the..."

Chaos. The entire day was chaos, and he had no words of wisdom. Where were all his years of experience with dealing with difficult situations?

She ran over the glass and checked behind the bookcase. Then under the television. "It's not here."

Confusion etched across her brows, but she sought Houston as if he could hold the answers. "Someone took the picture of my brother. It was the last one before Crispin left."

A thud came from outside. It sounded like a vehicle door closing near the side of the house.

Then an engine roared to life.

Her eyes widened. "They're still here."

Houston beat her to the front door and turned the knob.

She put her hand on top of his. "I have a gun in my closet."

No way was he letting her go outside without him. "You go get the gun. I'll check outside."

He opened the door in time to hear tires spinning on the loose gravel. He jumped down the steps and sprinted around the house. Headlights zeroed in on him.

The car barreled right toward him.

Houston leaped back, but the side passenger

mirror of the tan car clipped the edge of his bad hip. His body spun in the air, and he hit the ground.

Pain hammered through him as he rose to his hands and knees. Rocks bit into his palms. The ache was nothing like it had been in the past. Nothing like his burns. Not even close to his complications from the bone marrow donation to his brother. But of course it was the same hip.

He pushed himself up.

"Houston!" Sophie's hands landed on his shoulders. Then his cheeks. "Where are you hurt?"

Dust and gravel kicked back at them from the driveway. No brake lights from the tan car as it zipped down Sophie's drive.

Houston stood on his feet. A trickle of pain buzzed along his body. He took one step, then two. He'd borne much worse before. "I'm okay."

Or he would be.

He tightened his jaw and squinted through the dusty air, focusing on the car's license plate. "8Tw99m. Hurry and call that number in to the sher—"

"You call it in." Sophie placed her phone in his hand and took off for her truck. "I'm going to follow that car."

"You're going to what?" The car took a right onto the road, and Houston caught Sophie's arm as she turned for the truck. "Let the sheriff find him. He only took a picture of your brother."

Tears pooled in her eyes. "Yes, a picture of Crispin. Why? What if the reason there was no body of my brother for me to bury was because he's still alive? Somewhere. What if that person knows something? Somehow. Why would a burglar only take Crispin's picture from everything in my house?"

Her face paled and her eyes pleaded. She stood there awaiting an answer he didn't have.

He wanted to pull her against him. Hold her. Bring comfort. Instead, he moved his thumb over her skin. "Sophie..." He softened his tone for the girl who had begged him to do her portion of frog dissection. "Sometimes a body isn't returned because there may not be much left to send home."

She shook her head. "That first year he was gone, on Mother's Day, I got the first of yearly coded postcards. Stuff written that only Crispin would have known about. He can't be dead. It doesn't make sense."

She was right, it didn't.

Her arm shook under his touch. The look in her teary gaze was filled with fear and hope and pure stubbornness. She would follow that car with or without him.

And no way did she need to drive this upset.

He dropped his hand from her arm. "Let me drive?"

She stepped back and nodded.

"Keys in the ignition. I'll unhook the horse trailer."

Once she was buckled and on the phone with the sheriff, Houston floored the truck down her drive. Maybe by the time they reached the road, he'd have figured out if his heart raced from adrenaline. Or because of someone else.

Like the girl who trusted him enough to hop into the passenger seat of her own truck.

FIVE

Sophie squeezed the phone pressed up to her ear. "Sheriff, do I need to repeat the numbers or…?"

As her truck fishtailed around a corner, she pumped her right foot harder against the passenger side floorboard. If only Houston could drive both faster and slower all at the same time.

"Or do you…"

Her phone beeped in reply.

She held out her screen to see her fear revealed — no signal. A groan escaped her lips. "Can't something go right today?"

"I can still see the car up ahead. He hasn't gotten away." Houston's hand landed on top of her trembling fingers.

She took in a deep breath. The tension in her shoulders released a fraction. Maybe at least one thing had gone okay. If the break-in had to happen, maybe it wasn't the worst thing to have had Houston around.

He put his hand back on the wheel, and Sophie fisted her fingers. "So if this person may have known or worked with your brother, why would he track you down and take a picture?"

Should she tell him about what led her to change her name?

Instead, she shrugged. "Maybe there was something on the back of the picture that helps Crispin be found? I know that sounds crazy but..." She pointed to an angled tree with its branch stretching out ahead. "The road curves after that low branch."

"If I slow down..."

Then they might lose whoever had been in her house. Lose her chance at finding something out about her brother. "Don't slow down." There were too many unanswered questions at stake. "The only way any of this makes sense is if someone has made a connection between me and Crispin."

The truck caught air over the top of a hill, and her stomach seemed to bounce off the ceiling and back to her seat. When the tires hit the gravel again, Houston flinched. "I think now would be the perfect time to tell me why you go by Sophie instead of Rachel."

She closed her eyes. Of course he was right. She could hardly let the man drive her on a speeding chase and not know more.

Hadn't he proven himself to be trustworthy? "In one of the towns I lived in after Last Chance County, I thought I was followed one night after getting ice cream. I was in my mid-twenties. Crispin was off on another mission. I just thought it was my nerves getting to me. Then the next day, the same car caused me to wreck into a bridge. I got lucky. My ankle was the only thing that was broken. After Crispin returned home and found out what happened, he said it was no accident. Then he came up with the plan for me to change my name and to move again. That time, I moved to Wyoming."

Houston let off the gas. "You should have told me this first. The people we're chasing could be the people from back then. Sophie, you could be in danger."

She placed her useless phone in her lap. "I hope they are the same people and we stop them. I don't want to move and hide again. If we figure out who is after me or Crispin, I can finally be done with all this. I can finally have some answers."

He clenched his jaw, and his Adam's apple bobbed slowly.

The dimming sunshine sparked off the loose gravel country road ahead of them. Not exactly the ideal situation for a car chase. That and the fact her driver from out of town had probably never seen this road before.

They slid around a curve. Her hands braced against the door. The truck fishtailed until the back wheel hit the edge of the road. When they straightened, Houston grunted and leaned closer to the door, toward his left—the side that hadn't been hit by the car.

Oh, poor Houston. "Stop. We have to go the other way."

She'd only been worried about her home and the stolen photo. Meanwhile, Houston had been clipped by that tan car.

He sent her a side glare. "Got a shortcut?"

"Yes, straight to the hospital." She lifted the edge of his yellow Nomex shirt.

He winced. An angry, purple bruise formed a knot above his hip bone.

"See. You're hurt. Turn. Around."

He swatted her hand away and pushed the gas pedal down farther. The engine roared, and gravel on the road spit up and pinged against the underbelly of the truck. "I've been through much worse. This was nothing compared to after I donated bone marrow to Macon."

"Which only proves you'll risk your life for others. This is so not the time to be a stubborn hero." Her fingers touched the hem of his shirt. "Is there more above what I saw? I need to find out if you're bleeding. Being hurt in the past doesn't mean you're immune to it forever."

Before she could see the condition of his side, one of the front tires struck a pothole and bounced her in the seat. Houston's arm locked around her, pulling her tighter against his side. He grunted as he let off the gas.

As the truck slowed just before another turn, his face was right beside hers. "Please tighten your seatbelt."

"Please let me check your side?"

The truck steadied, and he punched the gas. "Does the road straighten after the next curve?"

She pressed her palm on the heated dashboard above the radio as they zoomed around the next bend. "I think there's a little incline and then a much bigger drop on the other side."

She lifted the bottom of his shirt, and Houston sucked in a breath.

His skin was puckered in places she assumed were

from the healed burns. A scrape about the size of her fist was above the bruise. No blood. And no bones seemed out of place.

"See, I'm fine." His knuckles paled around the steering wheel. "Like I said."

"Lying does neither of us any good. You could have internal damage."

"It's a bruise, Soph. Now tighten your seatbelt because you shouldn't be able to slide halfway across the bench."

Despite missing the feel of his shoulder against hers, she scooted over to the passenger side and pulled on the worn belt. "Happy?"

She wasn't.

Why had she only been thinking about herself?

He swerved the truck over to the far side of the incline. "Ask me that again later."

As the truck roared over the hill, the motion took her stomach, and she grabbed hold of Houston's leg.

The front tires returned to the ground and the shocks groaned. In front of them, the cloud of dust seemed more concentrated. But where was the car? They had to be catching up, and yet Houston braked down the hill.

"What are you doing?"

"Slowing down, so we don't end up like that." He pointed about half a mile up ahead.

She squinted through the air coated with dust and found brake lights. The reason she no longer saw the tan vehicle in front of them was because the car had flipped over on the side of the road. The metal underbelly portions of the car matched the gravel and dusty weeds.

"It looks like he was trying to take that path through the woods there."

A trail she'd never noticed before. One that might connect back to her ranch. "That path could be how someone buried the dead body."

"Yet another reason to wait for the sheriff."

"But he didn't hear where we were."

A hooded man crawled out of the broken side window of the tan car and sprinted for the woods beside the road.

Houston pulled the truck to the shoulder. She unbuckled and then opened the door and jumped out before Houston had completely stopped.

The shadowy form was tallish. For sure lanky. His hood fell back, revealing familiar dark hair on the young man's head. She knew who had broken into her house.

"Lewis!" She pumped her arms faster.

The teen darted off the path and into the trees. It could be one of the other boys Lewis shouldn't be hanging with, one with the same hair color, but she was ninety percent sure it was her best friend's nephew.

The truck door slammed behind her, but she kept her focus on Lewis's form as he weaved through the trees ahead of her.

Sticker bush branches scraped her arm, and she stumbled over a tree root. "Lewis. Stop!"

Up ahead, Lewis glanced back at her right before he jumped down into a dried riverbed.

A pile of withering leaves acted like a surfboard for Sophie's foot as she slid down to the bottom. "Lewis!"

Her boot hit only a trickle of water. Pieces of

driftwood, pine needles, and stones lined what was more than likely a creek only during the rainy season.

Lewis peered over his shoulder, but this time his foot struck one of the rocks half covered in leaves. Before he pushed himself all the way up, Sophie dove for him.

He'd taken her photo of Crispin. She didn't know why, but she was tired of him stealing from her.

She landed on his leg, and she wrapped her arms around his thigh. "Don't you move, Lewis. Marley is worried sick about you, and you're in a world of trouble. Why'd you break in? Why'd you steal my brother's picture off my wall?"

"I didn't break in." He rose onto one of his knees. "Never took a picture. I was only looking for my earbuds I'd lost one day with Peanut. Just let me go!"

The sheriff had been right. She should have filed a report on him for stealing money from her earlier. Maybe then he might not have caused this mess. But she had tried to lighten Marley's load.

When Lewis squirmed in her grip, something shiny around his throat caught her attention. She released her grip and grabbed hold of the necklace.

At the bottom of the chain was a pair of rings. A man's and a woman's. Both gold with one tiny diamond. She knew if she flipped the smaller one over, it would be engraved with a sunflower on the inside—her mother's favorite flower.

She gripped the necklace tighter. "W-where did you get this?"

That first postcard she'd received after her brother's death had said, *remember when we picked the neighbor's sunflowers?*

Only Crispin and Sophie had picked flowers for

Mother's Day only to get in trouble for it afterwards because they had cut down their neighbor's prized sunflowers.

"How..."

Lewis's widened eyes set on something behind her, and he slipped from her grasp, backpedaling on the ground.

Houston leaped from the top of the hill and bumped into Lewis, who somehow kept his feet. As the teen steadied himself on a tree trunk, Houston lunged and landed on top of Lewis.

Lewis wiggled underneath Houston's weight, but was no match for the man.

Houston sat up and sank his knee onto Lewis's chest. "Now would be a good time to answer her."

Lewis coughed and pushed his arms against Houston. "I didn't do it. I swear."

Sophie's numb feet stepped over to him, and she lifted the rings on the chain. "Where did you get *this* necklace? It wasn't in my house. I haven't seen it in three years."

Crispin.

He'd last had the necklace. But it had disappeared with her brother.

Her breath caught.

Houston lifted his body off of Lewis and helped him sit, keeping his hands around the boy's shirt. Lewis shook his head, and the chain slipped right into Sophie's hands.

With leaves sticking to his hoodie, he licked his chapped lips. "W-we found it in the woods."

Houston narrowed his eyes. "Where? By the squirrels you and your friends were—"

"B-by a body." His gaze bounced between

Houston and Sophie. "But we didn't kill him or bury him. We only found the body like that. I swear it."

Sophie's hands shook. Yes, they indeed looked like her parents' rings. The ones her brother wore to remind him of what truly mattered in the world. God and family.

Her legs froze beneath her. "You found this necklace by the burned body?"

Tears formed in her eyes. The body…She bit down on her quivering bottom lip. "That's why I haven't received a postcard yet this year. Because…"

"Sophie?" Houston blurred before her.

Her next step backward hit a softer section of ground, and her ankle twisted. Pain exploded up her leg. A cry ripped through her mouth as she fell.

She crashed onto the ground. Her knee knocked against something hard—a root or tree stump. Or just rock bottom.

Yet that wasn't what hurt the worst. Her brother might really be dead this time, and there was nothing she could do to save him. Like her parents, she had to figure out how to live after the dirt covered the grave that laid them to rest.

Why did God take away everyone she loved?

She groaned as her hands wrapped around her ankle. The one that never seemed to heal since the car accident. And before that, the earthquake.

Houston knelt over her. "Is it your leg? Ankle? Talk to me, Soph."

Sophie blinked. Houston's arms encircled her. She leaned into his chest.

But if Houston held her, then where was Lewis?

She shoved Houston's chest. "Where's Lewis? We've got to go get him."

Houston lowered his chin, blocking her view of Lewis's retreating form. "A hotshot does not abandon their crewmembers. I'm not leaving you alone when you're hurt."

A hot tear leaked from her eye. "Please, Houston." She pressed against his chest again. She needed answers. Needed closure. Needed help.

Houston wiped the tear from her cheek. "Is anything broken?"

Her eyes snapped to his. He didn't look away, only held her attention with those golden flakes that made her want to think of good things.

His fingers lightly grazed around hers and moved down her leg.

"No," she whispered. Lewis was gone, her brother could be the burned body, and then she would have no one left. "My ankle isn't broken."

But her heart was in pieces.

$\rightarrowtail\!\!\!\leftarrowtail$

Houston's heart hurt worse than his bruised hip. Sophie's tears made him want to take on her pain. But he couldn't. Life didn't exactly work that way. "Let's keep your boot on for compression. I don't think I have anything that will help you in my pack back at the truck, other than some pain reliever."

She placed one of her hands on his arm and lifted her trembling fingers, which held the necklace that Lewis had been wearing. "This was my brother's necklace. If Lewis found it by the burned body. That means..."

"The body could be your brother's." All Houston could do was wrap his arms around her.

She laid her forehead on his chest. Her tears were warm through his uniform. "How can Crispin be dead?"

He rubbed his fingertips up and down her back. "We don't know for sure if the body is your brother." Houston kept his voice steady. "There's still hope."

That's what he'd spent years teaching the youth group, that there's always hope. Hope in Christ. Which was still true—and always would be. But the past few months, with the trials he'd faced, God seemed farther away than ever.

Yet hope in Christ didn't mean there would be no more hardships.

Tears weaved around her lashes until her eyes popped back open. Her chest rose and fell as if she'd galloped away on Daisy.

Her hands went to her chest. "Every holiday I'd gotten a postcard that only he could have sent. Except this year. And now I know why." As her hand drifted from his to wrap around her hurt ankle, a silent sob quaked through her body.

And his heart.

A familiar sound rumbled in the distance. Something that sounded too much like Sophie's retro truck engine and the crunch of spinning wheels on gravel. Her vehicle was being stolen—leaving them stranded here.

Sophie released her ankle. "My truck!"

Houston's shoulders sagged, but he didn't lessen his grip from around her. "I left the keys…my pack. I never thought…Lewis must have circled back and taken it as his means of escape."

Houston should have kept a hold of the teen, but

Sophie had needed him more. He'd made the tough choice, and now they were alone out here.

"I'm sorry, Sophie." His mistake tasted like ash.

Wait.

He whipped his gaze around in the shadowed trees standing guard. Amongst the smoke snaking toward them, there was light in the distance. But it wasn't the sun. Flames rocketed up a tree branch that canopied the valley ahead. The smoky air hit his face and caused him to draw in an unsteady breath.

The wind had changed directions. Good for Sophie's ranch. Bad for their current location.

He scooped up Sophie in his arms. "We've got to move. Now. A dried-up valley is not the place we need to be."

She wrapped one of her arms around his neck, and the shift of the weight helped him take his next steps faster back up the incline. Her wide eyes were fixed on something over his shoulder. "Houston…"

A snap echoed in the woods, and Houston turned to see an ablaze overhanging branch drop into the dried riverbed.

Houston picked up his pace. His hip screamed at him to stop. But he couldn't. He was going to have to live through another fire.

Lord, where are You in this?

At least he had his fire shelter in his pocket.

A cough shook Sophie in his arms. "Let me down. I think I can put some weight on my ankle."

He flexed his arms around Sophie. They'd need all the speed they could get. "No, I've got you."

His scars on the back of his head and neck tickled as if they trembled at the heat coming for them. "That fire can travel uphill at sixty miles an hour. We've got to push hard to the road. It isn't that far." And it was a barrier that might slow down the fire. "At the very least, we can get under a shelter." Her eyes widened further at the sight behind him. "Oh—"

He didn't turn around. Didn't need to. He heard the sizzle of the sap. The hiss of flames consuming leaves. He squeezed his arms tighter around her, and she leaned into him as he ran toward their only hope.

He dodged the trees and lifted Sophie through the sticker bushes. Smoke entangled them. His eyes burned. He squinted. There. Finally. Ahead through the swaying branches, a clear path to the road.

He breathed through the pain in his hip. Smoke clung to his lungs. He could do this. They were going to make it. Then he spotted the tan car at the bottom of the hill. Houston slowed his pace. "I forgot about Lewis's flipped car."

"That car was not owned by Lewis or his aunt. Not that that's the point right now. Can you push it over?"

"Any other moment your faith in my strength would boost my ego, but no, not feeling any superhuman abilities presently. But that's not the problem." He veered off toward his right, where the road curved up ahead. His legs numbed with each step toward nowhere. "I failed to factor the car's gasoline tank into the fire barrier and survival equation. If the fire is moving as fast as the wind is whipping through the trees, the flames will light the gas and the explosion will probably reach us even in the fire shelter."

Her hands fisted around his shirt. "Your pack was in the truck. We don't have your fire shelter."

He quickened his strides. "It's in my pocket. We have to stay on the road, away from the fire load."

"English, please. What does fire load mean in firefighter language?" A cough thundered through her. It was hard to tell if the air was getting darker from smoke or from the setting sun. But her cough let him know exactly which.

Before he could answer, Houston's foot hit a raised root, and he stumbled.

Sophie gasped.

He stutter-stepped and found his balance. With a twinge of pain from his side, he pulled Sophie back up against his heaving chest. "I'm all right, are you?"

"Honestly?" Her word tickled against his neck. "I've actually been worse. Once. During an earthquake."

He wanted to ask when. Wanted to learn more about the woman Sophie had become. But instead, he said, "Then let's keep it that way."

After a few jogging steps, Sophie motioned toward the shadowed road in front of them that appeared to go straight off into the trees. "The road hooks hard up to the left. We should cut through the woods. It would save us time."

"We need to be on the road away from the debris that can catch fire when we deploy the fire shelter."

"But can't the hill act as another barrier for the fire?" Her voice had a calmness to it. No longer shaky. That made one of them.

"Yes. The flames might not jump across the gravel to the trees on the other side."

She met his gaze. "Then let's take the shortcut. We'll stay close to the road in case it comes time to deploy the fire shelter. Maybe we won't need it."

"Maybe." But he wasn't counting on it.

His second wind would come. It had to. Or they needed to take the shortcut and pray for the best.

He repositioned his tingling arms around Sophie. The wind whipped through the branches overhead, and a thick cloud of smoke blocked out any help from the sun.

Houston sucked in air and coughed.

Sophie placed her palm against his chest. "Let me down. My ankle isn't throbbing much right now."

"I'm sure you can walk, but I still think me carrying you will be faster."

"Houston, you're getting tired. It's that or we have to take the shortcut."

Sweat dripped down the back of his shirt as if to prove her observation.

Lord, what do we do?

Houston eyed Sophie's ankle. "Okay, we'll try the shortcut."

The only sound over the popping fire that filled the woods was his footsteps thumping on the ground, the wind, and his uneven breaths. His feet stepped even faster into the tree line on the opposite side of the road.

"Soph?"

"Hmm."

Ten more steps and they'd reach the top of the next hill. Then he could spot the curved road once more.

Inhale. Exhale. Sweat dripped into his eye. Sophie sagged against his chest. All except her arms that snaked around his neck, tightening. Another round of coughs rattled through her.

He needed to get her out of the smoky air. But that was hardly an option.

"Might have to nickname you python soon."

Her arms loosened. "Sorry."

Another cough coursed through his body, shaking him. His feet slowed. His next pant brought in more smoke than air.

She tapped his shoulder. "Hey, talk to me."

It was growing darker ahead of them, which meant the fire might be slowing down. Maybe they could keep hiking and not deploy the shelter. If only he had his walkie and could radio HQ for the fire's path.

Please, Lord. Please give me the easy way for once.

The toe of his boot whacked against a stump hidden in the leaves swirling on the ground, and he pitched forward. A yelp came from Sophie, and he released her legs in time for him to fall on his hands and not squish her.

He met the ground with a groan. His hip pain made him grit his teeth. He spat out a piece of dirt from his mouth. "You good?"

She scooted closer to him. "I think so."

He rolled over onto his back and waited for any further pain, but there wasn't any. His lungs squeezed. His side ached as if someone had given him an uppercut gut punch.

He pushed himself up. An ache quaked through his side. From their position on the hillside, he took in the horizon behind them. The fire had roared up the tallest pine tree. Its branches melting in the heated flames and dropping on anything that wasn't already aflame.

Another rookie mistake. He never should have left

the road. Now they were surrounded by trees and dead leaves and sticks. Perfect food for the hungry flames.

Disaster was coming, and unless God provided a miracle, whether Houston liked it or not, he was about to endure another fire. This time, he'd brought Sophie into his mess. And he'd picked the worst spot to have to deploy their only shelter.

SIX

Ash rained down, and reality struck Sophie on her cheek. They were going to die. "I never should have told you to take the shortcut."

But that wasn't the real reason death was knocking.

Houston grimaced as he used a nearby sapling to rise to his unsteady feet.

A cough rattled through Sophie, and she squeezed the necklace in her palm. "I shouldn't have told you to chase Lewis. Crispin is dead even though I longed for him not to be. And now the chances are high that we're going to end up the same way. I tried to do the right thing and help Lewis by giving him a job, and everything went terribly wrong."

Did God not see the good she had done?

Houston reached for her. "We're going to make it up to the road and deploy the shelter."

She took his hand and put some weight on her ankle. It didn't throb. Houston's breathing was brash and labored. She couldn't let him carry all the burdens. "Don't pick me up. I can run." Or at least hobble beside him. He didn't release his arm from around her side as they climbed the ridge.

Sophie licked her chapped lips. Her throat burned as if she'd spent all day riding in the sun without bringing her water pack.

A thunderous crash boomed in front of them. Sophie's entire body flinched.

Houston released her and dashed away, up the rest of the incline. And stopped at the peak of the plateau. Whatever he saw made him race back to her and scoop her up.

She heaved out a breath. "W-what is it?"

Another cough rattled through her. She tucked her nose in her shirt.

When they reached the top of the hill, it was like looking into a mirror of flames. Except the water tower peaked through the smoke before them.

Fire was behind them. And now in front of them. Surrounded.

Sophie gasped. "Now what?"

Houston tilted his head. "The road is just past that spruce ahead. We're going to beat the fire there."

All she could do was lean against her hero—the man who kept standing between her and the flames—and listen to his heart pound in his chest.

A tree branch scraped her arm and Sophie gritted her teeth.

They rounded the spruce tree, and as soon as Houston's boots hit the gravel road, she released her arms from around his neck.

He put her down and pulled something rectangular from his pocket. With a few flips of his wrists, the silver paper-looking tent unfolded.

Sophie glared at the object she did not want to place her hope in. "Please tell me that is the first layer of hundreds."

"Soph..."

Her chest tightened. This could not be happening. "I-I can't get in that."

It was teeny and didn't look thick enough to hold rain out, let alone fire.

Houston gave the tent another shake. "We're going to have to—"

"You don't understand. The earthquake." She shook her head. "I...They...My parents? We were trapped. They died. Now Crispin's dead and we're going to die in that tiny thing too."

He blinked up at her as if he understood. As if her pain and his were somehow connected.

"Trust me." His tone low. Yet strong. "This is the last thing I want to have to live through all over again. I'll be with you the entire time." His voice sounded muffled over the ringing in her ears—or was that the roar of the flames closing in on them?

Sophie stared at the fire shelter in Houston's hands. It resembled more of a piece of aluminum foil, ready to keep a pan clean. Not a lifesaving device. "How's that's supposed to protect us?"

"It's saved lives before."

She backed up until her shoulder hit a tree. "We have to keep going. We have to—"

"We can't, Sophie." He slipped his hand around hers. "The fire's encircled us."

"How?" Was all that made it out of her mouth before another cough cut her off.

How had God let it come to this?

Houston dropped to his knees and dug his fingers

into the rocky ground. "The fire must have jumped the road a way back. It probably ate up a tree, and it fell over the road just like it had in the riverbed. We have to take shelter. *Now.* We're completely surrounded, and the fire is going to roll over us whether we're ready or not."

She pulled up the neck of her shirt and covered her mouth and nose, her head as foggy as the ashy air.

Houston's fingernails were caked with dirt. "I should have been paying closer attention. I should have—I'm sorry, Sophie."

She yanked on his arm. "We've got to keep going."

But she didn't move him. He kept his head down, and he whispered something to himself—or to Sophie. She couldn't tell. Not even looking at the fire ahead that was closer than the one behind them. The road no longer separated them from anything. No, Houston wasn't speaking, he was humming a song. One she recognized.

It Is Well.

A hymn that every time they used to sing it at church when she was young, her mother had cried. But all was not well right now. Her ankle pulsed, and she panted as she gulped for clean air. But the smoke was everywhere. Death right around the corner.

"I don't want to die here." She tugged harder on his arm, but the man was a rock. One trying to save both their lives.

And what was she doing?

Now isn't the time to freak out. Even while the past knocked on the door of her heart and mind. Sophie had to keep it firmly locked away or she would get them both killed.

God, help us.

Finally, Houston stood. But instead of running, he raised the fire shelter.

"There's no more time to run." With a few motions, the so-called tent had grown, except it didn't look all that bigger. Or sturdier.

Her hands ran up her neck, then her cheeks, before she buried her face in her palms. Except squeezing her eyes shut didn't hide the memories of the confinement from the earthquake. Of also being trapped in the car accident.

Her good leg buckled beneath her, but something held her up.

Or rather, someone.

Worry lined Houston's creased forehead. "We're going to have to face the fire."

Face. Not run or hide. But she was so much better at the latter.

Her fingers latched on to the rings on the necklace around her neck.

Of course he was right. "W-what do I need to do?"

"Use one of those rocks to dig a hole in the dirt. You're going to make us a bigger air pocket." Houston's words came out staccato. "And tell me about the earthquake."

Her mind flew back to the first aftershock. The one that had completely trapped her. "My parents had told me to climb out my window. But I couldn't."

Houston slipped his hand into hers. "Let's kneel. I'm sure your ankle is throbbing?"

She tightened her fingers around his. "Don't trap me in that—"

"We're only kneeling."

Her body seemed to move when his did.

He let go of her hand as they both squatted onto their knees. "Now, we're going to lie down over that hole in the dirt so we can breathe better. The smoke will go over us, and we'll have clean air to breathe."

The fire popped in the distance, and she pressed her stomach against the bumpy ground. The loose gravel bit into her hips. The freshly dug dirt was cool against her palms, but her cheeks were flush. "Houston…"

She sealed her mouth closed. She didn't want to throw up.

He rested his hand on top of hers which had fisted on top of the ground. His eyes filled with a peace she didn't feel. Then he grimaced.

She frowned. "That's your bad side. You need—"

"Soph." His whisper made her stop. "This is the way of escape God has given us. I'd have chosen a different way, but He doesn't always listen to my plans."

"Surely there's got to be another way?"

He panted twice. His next breath was as loud as Sophie's fears. "The road won't allow the fire to go underneath us. And I need to shield you because I have the heat protective clothes on."

At his pause, her pulse beat harder, which did not help her throbbing ankle. But it did help her think. "And then the fire shelter?"

"Then the shelter, yes. I'll be with you the entire time. And Sophie, God is always with us."

He sounded so calm. How could he be so still when she was panicking? Yes, God would be with them, but that didn't mean they wouldn't be killed. "How will you get fresh air if you're on top—"

"To keep the fire shelter on, I have to slide my

arms through a section and put my boots and body on the inside flaps. I have to hold it tight to the ground."

Her empty fingers clawed at the pile of dirt from the dug hole. Didn't they need larger air holes to survive? She wouldn't allow him to shield her by giving up his life. He had been her protector every step of the way. Even when she didn't know she needed him.

But God had known.

Houston moved closer and rested his head against hers. "Don't think of it as being trapped. Think of it as surviving."

Surviving. Not trapped.

Her parents might have survived if she'd listened to their instructions. If she'd fought harder to get out. She had to listen to Houston now.

The man God had brought here to save her life.

"Can I slide my arm through one side and you can do the opposite? I know that thing's not big, but we both need to do this together. We used to work well together. Remember? You dissected all the frogs for me, and I wrote out our essay."

A brief smile, and then, "We can't this time. You'll get burned if your arm is in the pockets instead of mine." Houston shot up and positioned the fire shelter over her before she could abort the mission. "You're going to have to trust, Sophie."

Darkness slipped around her. "Houston!"

"I'm right here," he whispered.

She leaned further against him, and he seemed to do the same. She exhaled slowly through her mouth. They were going to make it. She only had to trust in God's ways.

And then a ripping sound obliterated her hope.

Too much light entered their once dark cocoon. How close were the flames now? Sophie glanced over her shoulder. The supposed survival tent had a tear down the middle. "I take it back! We can be trapped. We just need…"

She reached for both ends of the fire shelter. Except the two separate fire tent pieces were not going back together.

It had torn down the center. "No, no—"

Houston's palms rested on either side of her cheeks. "New plan."

However, his eyes darted around, not meeting her gaze.

Her stomach clenched.

He didn't have another plan.

Sophie threw down the broken fire shelter. "How about we keep running and pray that the fire splits like the Red Sea."

What had Moses prayed that God told him to raise his staff so the sea would be parted?

Houston took a deep breath, then held out his hand to her. "Are you running or riding?"

She placed her hand in his, and he pulled her to her feet. "Running. I'm going to carry my own weight."

They moved toward their one o'clock. Left foot. Right. The fire in front of them was darkened by the haze. A crackle of the fire snapped louder. Closer. But in which direction? Probably all of them.

"How long before…"

The fire caught up with them?

How long before they burned to death?

"Truth?" Houston coughed. "Pray that your Red Sea fire miracle will be sooner rather than later."

Fire. The last way Houston ever wanted to die. Though none of the options were on today's to-do list. If given a choice, going up like Elijah might be his preferred way to go, eventually. But without the flames on the chariot and many, many years from now.

Houston squeezed his fingers around Sophie's side. Even with her limp, Sophie kept a steady pace.

"If we don't make it. I'm…" She swallowed and turned her gaze on him. Soot and dirt mixed with fear streaked across her face. "I'm not sure what I would've done without you today."

Lord, why did You let the fire shelter rip?

Houston opened his mouth, but a loud whooshing noise thundered over the crackle of the flames snapping at their heels. A helicopter. It had to be.

His feet stuttered. Then a half laugh, mostly cough escaped. "A miracle helicopter."

Sophie wrapped her arm tighter around his back as if to hold him up. "A helicopter can get us out of here, right?"

Houston spun around. Tree branches formed a blanket above them. The smoke camouflaged them, and flames blocked an escape route toward any open ground.

The thumping noise escalated with the beat of his heart. "Not right here. But maybe up the road."

And that's when the helicopter flew overhead with a monsoon bucket.

"This may be the start of our parted Red Sea miracle. But we've got to get to some kind of barrier against the water." Houston slipped his hand into hers and pulled her toward the largest tree within a few steps. Branches stretched out from its base like a protective mother hen. "The crew's about to drop over two thousand gallons of water and fire-retardant foam. We need to get under as much shelter as possible. After the water hits, we'll run and try to get the pilot's attention in the open."

"And the fire?" Sophie whispered.

Houston kept his attention on the tree ahead, not the choking smoke or the flames brightening around them. All he could offer was a nod.

They reached the pine and ducked under the low-hanging branches. "Get as close to the trunk as possible."

She sank her elbows into the dirt and crawled forward until she put her back toward the trunk. Houston lowered onto his hands and knees. He placed his body next to hers and adjusted his ribs to lift his throbbing hip off the ground.

Sophie tucked her head closer to his chest. "How close do you think the helicopter is now?"

"Hopefully, it's swinging back around."

"Why is waiting so hard?"

Houston shoved a pine cone out from under his shoulder. "Before today, I thought waiting on my seminary acceptance letter had been taking forever."

But trials had a way of revealing the truth.

She tilted her face toward him. Her palm rested on his chest. "I remember when I was in fifth grade and my gym teacher would make everyone run for five minutes at the start of each class. It used to feel like an eternity. Kind of like waiting on a lifesaving helicopter filled with water."

Her voice quivered.

He needed to keep her talking. "Where were you in fifth grade?"

"California." She exhaled a shaky breath. "Was there until seventh grade. Then after the earthquake and aftershock where my parents died, Crispin and I bounced around a bit. He was only five years older than me, barely legal to take custody."

The whoosh of the helicopter had faded to the snaps of the fire. Houston closed his eyes. "I can't imagine being eighteen and having to be responsible for another. At that age, I'd failed my own life choices and spent months in the hospital recovering from the fire. But those days were where God changed my life, so I can't regret them."

Where Houston promised himself that he'd use his life for God's work.

He pulled a leaf out of Sophie's hair. "And where did you go after Last Chance County?"

"Nevada. Idaho. Then Crispin left and never came home. Last year I was still working in Wyoming, and I got a phone call. A lawyer said I'd inherited a ranch in Montana—a state I'd never even lived in."

She moved against him, probably from a shrug. "I thought…" Her voice hitched. "I thought it was Crispin somehow trying to take care of me despite being gone. That was until his postcards stopped. And I'd kept hoping the mail was only late." She sniffed and then wiped her cheek with her knuckles. "You though, you stayed in Last Chance County?"

He used his thumb to wipe away her stray tear. "Why leave when I had the perfect job?"

Until it wasn't.

Sophie ran her fingertips along the trail of his scar

on his wrist. "I had the greatest job in Wyoming. Planned to stay on that ranch working with the best thoroughbreds forever. Even thought I'd found someone to marry. But Landon kept wanting to sneak in and ride one of the racehorses. I had vetoed the idea, multiple times, but apparently not firmly enough. My now ex hopped on one of the most prized horses when I wasn't looking and took him out in the dark. The horse ended up stepping in a ditch. Broke two legs."

Sophie sniffed. "The horse had to be put down. Then when the authorities came, Landon said I allowed him to take the ride so he wouldn't be sued. I lost my job. I should have seen it coming, but…"

Houston had been there. Swimming in the whys.

"Soph, we're going to get out of this." Then he thought of the old hymn he'd first heard when he had awoken in the hospital, his body screaming from the burns. He murmured the lyrics, and Sophie laced her fingers with his.

Only the low hum of the flames was picked up in his ears over the song. Or was it the helicopter? God could have shifted the winds and changed the fire's course, but they probably would have noticed the movement in the branches above.

He didn't know whether he or Sophie moved closer, but their lips were only an inch away. His history with women since his burns had been disastrous. But technically, he'd met Sophie before his wounds. Would that make a difference?

As he lifted his hand to her cheek, a bang rocked through the air. Then the ground vibrated beneath them.

Sophie screamed, and Houston pulled her toward

him, wrapping his arms around her. This was not how he thought things would go.

Just as quickly, the ground stopped rumbling.

Sophie dug her nails into his hand. "What was that?"

"It could have been the monsoon water drop. Or it could even have been that car exploding." Which would mean the fire was growing stronger. Not weakening.

"It rumbled like an earthquake." Her body quaked under his touch.

"Are you…"

But he didn't get to ask if she was okay. Suddenly, water crashed into them. Anything that was fire's enemy should have been welcome at the moment. Instead, the coolness stole his breath and sent their bodies tumbling down the sloped land. He locked his fingers around Sophie's shirt as the water rolled her in a circle.

The swift current took them down the path they'd only just climbed up. Saplings and bushes grated against his skin as they slid by. She turned and reached for him.

Houston tugged her against him. The water wasn't too deep. They needed stand. Had to get steady before the water hurt Sophie's ankle even more. He placed his heel against the slick ground, but a floating stick poked him in his injured hip.

He jerked, and his head smacked against a tree trunk, slowing his descent until his body crashed up against another tree. Stars lit up his vision. His hands cradled his temple. When he pulled his fingers back, there was no blood. But something was far worse.

His grip was empty. "Sophie!"

Only the hiss of the dying flames and the thump of the helicopter's blades hit his ears.

He jumped to his feet and chased after the current. Down the rest of the angled terrain. The weeds were mowed over and sticks were piled against tree trunks. A rotted fallen tree had been caught up against something like driftwood. Wait. Was that the tan flipped car?

They were actually right back where they started.

Or at least Houston was. "Sophie!"

Please, God! I need her to be okay.

He spun back toward the hill they'd slid down in the impromptu water slide. Had she held tight to a sapling somewhere between the first plateau and valley?

"Houston." Her voice was weak.

Houston glanced over his shoulder. Nothing but foggy air that seemed to distort his ability to pinpoint her direction.

He stomped through the soggy ground before him. But she wasn't sitting or standing anywhere on the road. Wasn't clinging to a tree behind him.

God, where was she? "Sophie!"

The flames no longer trailed his every movement. The water had cut the fire off by soaking the ground around him. But he still needed to be mindful of the smoke smoldering up like a fence.

Footsteps splashing in a puddle allowed him to breathe again. He ran toward the sound to his left. "Sophie."

"I'm here." She rounded a tree.

Standing with mud-caked clothes, her wet hair stuck to the side of her cheek, and soot surrounded her haggard-looking eyes. He'd never seen anything more beautiful.

She limped toward him, but he was faster, and he wrapped his arms around her. She tucked her head against his chest. For a moment, the chaos around them stilled as he breathed her in.

Her touch against his shirt warmed his skin and his heart. They were drenched and drained, but not dead. He didn't want to move.

All too soon, he pulled back. His hands went to her arms. Her cheeks. Then he squatted and touched her ankle. "Anything else hurt worse?"

"I think I'm okay. And I think..." She rested her palms on his shoulders. "That maybe we've had enough character building for one day."

He rose slowly. "I'm sorry I let you go."

"No, I should have held on tighter. You already did more than your share when you had to carry me. You shouldn't have to protect me all the time."

His gaze locked onto hers. "Maybe I want to be the one who protects you."

Yes, he'd finally said what he'd been thinking all day.

She opened her mouth, but he didn't know what she was going to say. The roar of the helicopter made her look away. It circled overhead. One of the smokejumpers leaned out of the open door and pointed toward the road back to his right.

Just beyond the location of the flipped car, up on top of the hill, the trees were spread far enough apart where the helicopter could get a rope down to them.

He glanced down at Sophie, but he didn't have to say a word.

She'd already slipped her hand in his. "No more waiting. Let's go get rescued for the last time."

No more waiting. Except, once again, his timing wasn't right. She was staying—her life was here.

This was a summer gig, not his forever ending.

But maybe God had answered his prayer—he'd made things right. And that would have to be enough. Somehow.

SEVEN

"WHICH ONE OF YOU WOULD LIKE TO GO FIRST?" Dark circles had burrowed under the sheriff's eyes, and it didn't seem as if he was interested in any quips.

Too bad never wasn't an option. She'd much rather seal the past up and be done with it. Sophie tugged the blanket tighter around her shoulders. The scratchy fabric did little to warm the bleak white walls of the borrowed office.

Houston sat in the seat beside her in a fresh hotshot uniform. She had also showered and been given dry clothes, a protein bar, and a place to stay the night. One of the other female smokejumpers had even wrapped Sophie's injured ankle. Jude County Fire Headquarters had finer service than some motels she and her brother used to visit when they arrived in a new town.

Crispin.

She'd never again get to go anywhere with him. She slid her father's ring on the necklace around her thumb. The clock on the wall behind the sheriff blurred in her watery vision. It ticked off another second, announcing it was officially past the evening time to check on her horses. She needed to get home and see if they were okay. Life turmoil or not.

Houston crossed his legs underneath his chair. "We had returned to Sophie's ranch after we last saw you. When we got there, her house had been looted."

Sophie scooted forward in her seat. "More like ransacked."

She didn't want the sheriff to forbid her to return. She could still sleep there, broken windows or not. She only needed a ride. Hopefully, her truck would be found all in one piece. She would need every bit of her savings to afford the down payment for her barn loan if it ever got approved. "I don't know if he stole anything else yet, but he did take a picture of my brother." Her voice hitched on the last word.

Houston rested his hand on her leg. She met his concerned gaze.

Why did this man always seem to know what she needed? After what they'd been through, she wasn't surprised. Her chest squeezed, and she covered it with her palm.

It seemed God was fixated on taking those she cared for away. Her parents. Crispin. What if she'd lost Houston today too? It had been her mess that he'd chased her through.

Houston pulled his hand away all too soon. "We followed the suspect in Sophie's truck. It was Lewis."

She lifted the necklace in her hand. The cool chain coiled around her fingers. "When we caught up with Lewis…" Her throat scratched as she swallowed. "His comment…I now believe the burned body we found may be my brother Crispin."

The sheriff's eyes didn't widen in surprise. His

gaze simply bounced between her and Houston. "What led you to that conclusion?"

Sophie ran her thumb over the silver chain. "Lewis had my brother's necklace."

Houston moved his knee against Sophie's. "He claimed he found it near the body."

The sheriff lowered his palm-sized notebook. "Could it not be a similar necklace?"

If only. She clasped the rings in her fist. "These are my parents' rings on a chain."

Now that made the sheriff lean his elbows on the desk. "I will let you identify the body, but the medical examiner is still working. Though, I'm sorry to tell you, he said there's not much to go on right now. But unofficially, the coroner did mention that it looks like the body might have been shot before he was burned."

Sophie cradled the necklace against her chest.

Houston sat up straight. "Shot. You're sure?"

The sheriff nodded.

She'd believed murder was likely, given where and how they'd found the body. But someone had shot her brother and then burned him—burying him in the path of the fire to leave no trace. What kind of jobs had the government gotten her brother involved in?

No wonder he'd insisted she change her name.

"Do you know anyone who might want to hurt your brother?" The sheriff's phone rang in his pocket. He reached in and silenced it.

Sophie sniffed. "He worked for Homeland Security. But they said he died three years ago."

"I see." The sheriff ignored his vibrating phone again and made a note in his notebook.

A knock sounded on the office door as it cracked open. A dark-headed man with a stern expression leaned inside. "Excuse me, Sheriff Hutchinson, when you're done, I need Houston."

The sheriff put his hat back on his head. "I can talk with him more tomorrow if you need him now, Miles."

Commander Dafoe hooked his thumb over his shoulder. "My office."

Except Houston didn't rise. His eyes sought Sophie's. His brown eyes were both a hug and a gut punch. It would be too easy to lean into Houston's strength. How much she'd wanted to kiss him earlier, before their rescue. However, she needed to be able to deal with her mess of a life. He wouldn't be around forever. His dreams were not here in Ember.

She needed to let him go. Now. Before it hurt worse.

"Thanks, Houston, for everything." She gave him what she prayed was at least a half smile and balled the edge of the blanket in her hands.

Houston's Adam's apple bobbed.

Sophie dropped her gaze to the armrests separating them.

His commander opened the door wider, and the door groaned, stealing Houston's focus. Finally, he filed out of the room, and she suddenly wished she had a thicker blanket.

The sheriff's phone buzzed once more, and this time, he answered. "Hutchinson...yes." His gaze assessed Sophie. "She is...just a moment." He extended the phone across the desk. "For you."

Someone was calling for her. On the sheriff's phone? The blanket slipped from around her shoulders. Had the sheriff already texted the coroner? Was it time for her to identify the body?

Her trembling hand refused to reach for the phone. She changed her mind. She wasn't ready to know for sure if the body was Crispin. A sliver of hope was better than none at all. "Is it...the coroner?"

The sheriff gave her a fatherly expression. He covered the microphone portion of the phone. "It's someone else who cares for you. But if you wouldn't mind softening the blow about what all I have to tell her about Lewis, I'd appreciate it."

Marley. Of course. She'd probably called everyone in town after Sophie didn't show up for dinner. And Sophie's own phone was currently resting in a bag of rice in the HQ's main kitchen, trying to win the fight against the water that saved Sophie and Houston from the flames. Her phone was looking at a fifty-fifty chance of survival.

The sheriff shut the door behind him, and Sophie cradled the phone. "Hey, Marley."

"I totally need to hug you right now," Marley's voice rippled through the borrowed phone.

Sophie rested her elbow on the desk in front of her. "And I could totally take you up on that offer."

Or maybe relive the hug she'd gotten from Houston before she was whisked from him when the helicopter landed.

"What happened? Betty somehow got a video off someone's phone of you and that hotshot being rescued, and it's on the town's social media page. Had to do a double take. How did you end up back at the fire? You had evacuated. I saw you. Talked to you. You were safe. We were supposed to have dinner. Then you never showed, and I called and called."

Sophie inhaled slowly. She needed to be the one to tell her friend about Lewis instead of the sheriff. "Marley." She cleared her dry throat and spilled everything that she and Houston had told the sheriff.

After a pause of five of Sophie's heartbeats, a sigh over the speaker made Sophie's own shoulders slump. "I can't believe Lewis did…maybe he's not telling the truth. Or there's an explanation about your brother's necklace. You don't know for sure it's his. The police will be able to tell who the body is, right? I don't want you to fear the worst until we find out for sure."

Sophie wiped a hot tear off her cheek. "I'm not sure of anything right now."

At least that was the truth.

A shaky breath flew from her mouth. "All I know is, first my ranch almost burned down. Then my brother's gone. On top of that, I also almost got Houston and myself killed. And God…He…He must be so against me right now."

"Oh, honey. But He's not. I promise. Okay, I really need to give you that hug. Let me finish up with your horses at your house, and I'll be right where you are. But you have to tell me where that is. I broke down and called Betty Adams. She's how I got the sheriff's cell phone number. I had to listen to why I need to always keep red tulips in stock—maybe not the wisest person to call, but it was the quickest method. And I highly doubt you're at the sheriff's office because I already tried that number. Five times."

There was so much of that conversation that needed explaining, especially the repercussions of giving Betty any further gossip fodder. But that wasn't what came out of Sophie's mouth. "You took my horses out of their trailer?"

"Girl, those three are good and safe in your barn. Peanut was even a sweet angel. Now where are you?"

"I'm at the hotshot's headquarters. They said I could sleep here, but—"

"Yes, girl. Do that. Sleep. No more thinking. No more worrying. Your horses are good. You're alive. And so is Houston. Which by the way that man looked at you on the video, I don't think he's holding a grudge over being rescued with you."

"You didn't see his boss storm in here. What if he gets in trouble or loses his job or something because I—"

"Don't let yourself think that you can mess up so much that you can ruin God's plans. I don't understand all that He does, but He knows the bigger picture. I don't know what I'm going to do with Lewis. But this is proof that maybe it's a good thing we're getting away from those boys so soon. Not that that's an excuse. I'm so sorry, Soph, for his actions."

Sophie rubbed her temples. Her friend was right. She couldn't mess up God's plans, but why did some of His plans seem to be the opposite of what Sophie saw as good?

Wait. There had been a *we* in Marley's sentence.

Sophie moved to the edge of her seat. "Mar, what do you mean you're both getting away from those boys?"

The silence over the phone made Sophie draw her knees up onto the chair. This was not going to be good.

"Why don't we talk about this later. You've been through enough already."

"If it's bad news, there's never an ideal moment, no matter the time frame." Sophie wrapped the blanket around her and laid her chin on her knees. "I'm not going to sleep until you tell me."

A heavy groan and then, "Brady proposed."

"Oh, Marley, that's—"

"He wants me and Lewis to move to his hometown and stay with his sister until the wedding."

Oh, no…

"I know I'll be hours away, but Sophie that doesn't mean I'm ditching you."

Except it did kind of mean that. She was back to being alone. This was why Sophie did better with horses than people. Horses wanted to be around her.

"I know so much has happened tonight, and my leaving town soon isn't helping things. But I'm still going to be here for you, and if you get anything out of my move, it's that love is worth it. Give God a chance to see how He planned your life. It might surprise you what He does."

Sophie slipped her brother's necklace into the pocket of her borrowed jacket. Maybe. But so far, God's surprises hadn't been all that great. Except for the ranch and rescue helicopter.

And Houston. But could she fully allow someone else into her inner circle just to say goodbye again?

If only Houston could have protected Sophie more. But one can't shield someone from sadness. Not completely. She'd rested against him on the helicopter flight, but while talking to the sheriff, she had pulled away. Guarding herself. Her heart. Something

Houston himself had nearly perfected. Or so he'd thought, until Sophie crashed back into his life. But maybe it was for the best. He would be leaving at the end of summer.

Inside his office, Commander Dafoe shut the door and gestured to the chair in front of his desk. His eyebrows hung low in a stern expression. "Have a seat. I want to hear about everything since you were called out this morning."

Had it really only been a day? "How is the crew? Please tell me no one else got caught up in the fire?"

Commander Dafoe shook his head. "Thankfully no. Your crew had the fire controlled around Sophie's ranch. However, on another country road over, flames popped up out of nowhere. It's possible an animal could have turned over a burning barrel that still had hot coals, or it could have been those teens in the woods you and Price tried to flush out. Or something else entirely. Either way, flames escalated before we could get anyone over there. Now, I'm hoping your story might provide some more intel."

After a deep breath, Houston began with digging the line. Then explained about Lewis, Finn, and Preston in the woods, all the way to the car chase, and stopped at the monsoon dump.

Miles had his hands steepled in front of his mouth. "It wasn't only our water that dashed the fire around you and Sophie. The fire burned through one of the water tower's legs, and it crashed over."

Houston crossed his arms. His bruised hip knocked into the armrest, and he sucked in a breath. "That's the boom we felt." That's why there had been such a current and why Sophie had been ripped from him.

Miles leaned back in his chair. "You both were either in a lot of right places or a lot of wrong ones. It had been chance that the pilot saw you two when he did through all the tree coverage." He tilted his chin. "Though we know it wasn't chance."

"No, sir." God had performed many miracles today. Houston just wasn't sure what to do now. Nothing was going as planned.

Miles thumped his knuckles on his desk. "However, Price voiced a concern that we need to talk through."

Houston gripped the chair rests. He knew exactly what Price had brought to Miles's attention. "Sir, I hesitated when the firecrackers or the cigarette lit that brush fire with the youth. But it won't happen twice."

Miles picked up a pen and clicked it. "With your history with fire, it's only natural to have lingering fears. I just need to know if it's going to put the crew in danger. You included."

The safety of the team depended on his reaction time. Houston laced his fingers together and squeezed. Had his brother been right? Should he not have accepted this job?

Sophie's face came to mind. He had been there for her. Helped rescue her. Wasn't that what God wanted him to do? Save people physically, as a firefighter, and soon again, spiritually, as a church leader?

Miles pointed the pen at Houston. "Why do you want to be a hotshot?"

Houston pushed his shoulders back. "To be honest, sir, originally it was a combination of being fired from my other job and to also prove to my fire chief brother that I could. I'd believed the opened door here was a type of sign to help me finance my upcoming seminary education. But I want to help others avoid what I survived."

Miles set the pen down. "You are a fine rookie hotshot. But this team needs you at your best. So, if you can't handle—"

"I only need a night's sleep."

Miles narrowed his eyes. "Have a doctor check out your hip. And I suggest finding someone wise to talk through today and the future with."

"Sir, I know I want to be a hotshot and attend seminary."

Miles held up his palm. "Not exactly that future I was talking about."

Houston tilted his head. What else was there? "Sir?"

Miles stood. "Just be careful. I caught a glimpse of what the social media page posted. Those we rescue sometimes fall for the hero moment, not the man."

Houston ran his hand over his bald head. Was he saying that he thought Sophie had fallen for him? Or at least for the idea of a hero? Based on his track record with women, and Sophie's see-you-around comment, unfortunately the commander had nothing to worry about in that department. "Sophie and I knew each other from high school, is all."

The commander grunted. "Get some rest. You're currently on the clock in the morning, but we can make do without you. If—"

"I'll be ready." Houston hustled out of the office, and his legs carried him back to where the sheriff and Sophie had been. But before he could knock on the door, his phone rang. The phone he had been glad he'd left in his locker—or it would be trying to dry out like Sophie's.

A number he didn't recognize filled the screen.

He swiped, then said a rushed, "Hello."

"Oh, hey, uh, Houston." The familiar voice sounded breathy. Panicked. "I thought you'd be busy, fighting that wildfire. I heard about it on the news, and I just thought I'd leave a message."

Wait. "Elijah?"

A pause and then, "Yeah, yes, hey, it's me. I, ah... is this a bad time?"

Would it ever be a good time to speak to the man who replaced him as youth pastor? Houston clenched his fingers. He glanced down the hallway. No one to witness his awkwardness. "What's up, Eli?"

A sigh heaved through the phone's speaker. "How did you do it?"

Houston leaned his shoulder against the wall, his focus on the door where he'd left Sophie behind. "Do what?"

"Get through to the youth group. They don't listen to me like I know they listened to you."

Houston exhaled through his nose. Did the man mean to be tempting Houston with something he couldn't have?

Eli kept going, "Ava's stopped coming regularly. Leighton's too busy flirting her lashes at Gabe to give any respectable answers to my lesson questions. Belle Harte's mom keeps calling...I believe you, by the way. I overheard Belle talking, and she told Nicole she wasn't even there the day you went to help her mom move furniture. She said her mom had even lied about other men in other towns too. That means we can prove you didn't do what Mrs. Harte implied about how you came on to her, because there are others like you. The church elders shouldn't have let you go based on that woman's word."

Eli believed that he hadn't flirted inappropriately with Mrs. Harte, but only after he'd overheard Belle. Even if the elders believed him now, they had already demoted Houston because he didn't have Eli's fancy degree. But he would one day soon.

Houston stared at the fluorescent light humming on the ceiling. A part of him wanted Eli to continue to fail. To prove to the church that they had gotten it wrong by hiring him instead of Houston. But that would do the kids no good.

Houston rested his forearm up against the wall. "It takes time to build a relationship. Just keep showing up. Not only at church, but at their games, plays, birthday parties, and generally in their lives. Keep sharing God's truth. Don't waver. Remember that all you can do is plant the seeds of Truth. Be faithful to water those seeds. God is the one who makes it grow in their lives."

"You make it sound so easy. I *thought* it would be easy. Maybe because you made it look that way growing up."

Houston relaxed his fingers out of their fists. "Looks can be deceiving. If you need help...I'm here."

"That's part of the problem. You're actually there. Not here. But thanks, and also...I, uh, accidentally opened mail that was yours. It was addressed to the church and had my alma mater on the return label, and I assumed...I guess I didn't look at the name, and then I'd already read your mail before I realized what I'd done."

Eli's alma mater was Truth Seminary.

Finally, news about Houston's application. "No worries."

The pause made Houston's heart rate climb.

"Sorry, Houston," Eli's voice mumbled. "But you didn't get in. There was some discrepancy with your references."

Houston hung his head. Of course his references had been contacted *after* the situation with Mrs. Harte.

God had closed another door on Houston's plans. How was Houston supposed to make a difference in people's lives if God kept shutting doors? He squeezed his eyes shut.

"I can give them a call." Eli rambled on. "Maybe the truth will come out now. I can talk to Belle —"

"Thanks, Eli, but no." No, he didn't want his name dragged further through the mud, and there was no way to know that Belle wouldn't lie again for her mother. "I've got to go. Thanks for letting me know."

Now what was he supposed to do?

Someone cleared their throat from behind Houston.

Houston turned around to find Logan, Macon's best friend, who helped get Houston a job as a hotshot. His hair was styled with gel and his dark-wash jeans and black polo made him look more ready for a date than clocking in.

"Hey, Houston, sorry, man." He lifted a packet of papers up that he probably needed to drop off at the chief's desk. "I'll blame it on the small hallway. Plus, I hadn't realized you were on a private call."

"It's fine, Logan." More than likely, he heard nearly every word. "At least I don't have to give you Cliffs Notes." Or pass it to his brother.

"I know you're upset about how things went down in Last Chance County, rightly so, but maybe you wouldn't have left otherwise. I know I wouldn't have if..." He shrugged without finishing what he was avoiding in Last Chance County.

"That's one way to look at it." Houston pocketed his phone.

Logan marched around him and knocked on the chief's door, then opened it.

But it was empty. No sheriff. No Sophie.

Logan stepped past Houston and lifted something off the armrest of the chair Sophie had been sitting in. Something silver. "Someone's going to be missing this."

Houston's stomach tightened. "I know who that belongs to." How had she forgotten that after all they went through?

Logan held it out, and Houston grabbed the necklace. "If it's the woman with the sheriff, I think they just left. Heard something about her truck being located."

Lewis must have ditched it. Houston put the necklace over his head. "Do you know where they found her truck?"

Logan wrinkled his nose and then set the paper down on the chief's desk. "I want to say over by the movie film set."

"Thanks, Logan." Houston sprinted down the hallway.

"You might want to answer one of your brother's texts. He messaged me about you," Logan shouted at Houston's back.

Sounded about right.

Footsteps thumped after Houston as Logan

caught up. "You know that your brother...You should know he said he was proud of you."

Houston slowed to a walk and raised his brows. He'd stopped him for this? Macon had left a message on Houston's phone when he and Sophie had gotten back to HQ. Never once mentioned any of those words. "I really got to —"

"Seriously, Houston. He may not tell you with those exact words. He's still a bit blinded by his opinion that you're running away, but..."

Houston's back stiffened. "Running away? They let me go. I was forced to find a new job. So I did."

There was that word again: *I*. Had he spent enough time praying about his decisions?

Did Macon have a point?

Logan thumped him on the shoulder. "I'm not arguing with you. That was supposed to come out as a compliment. Apparently, it sounded better in my head."

"Apparently." Houston lifted the necklace, and Logan waved him on.

He grabbed his truck keys from his locker. He didn't know why Lewis would be out near the film set, but Sophie would be worried about the last thing she had of her brother's. He'd eventually talk to Macon. But for now, Sophie needed her necklace. And hopefully, she still needed Houston a little too.

Maybe not getting into seminary wasn't the worst thing that could happen to him. But a broken heart might be.

EIGHT

"You're sure you're good?" The sheriff's headlights reflected the doubt in the man's eyes.

Today would never be a good day. But she still had something to be thankful for. Her truck. It was found parked crooked with the back half on the curve of the road heading to the movie set. The keys still hung in the ignition. If she'd been counting the day's answered prayers, God had been showing up. Which had to prove that He still cared for her.

Sophie threw her jack and tire iron wrench into the back of her truck. "I'm going to make it. Thanks for helping me with this."

The moonlight sprinkled down through the branches, forming a pergola effect over the road. "I appreciate you driving me out here and helping me change the two blown tires."

No wonder Lewis had ditched her truck. But what had the boy been thinking leaving her and Houston in the woods? Maybe he hadn't known about the fire pressing in. More than likely, he'd been scared of getting in trouble, and he fled without thinking.

She didn't want to, but she could sympathize with that gut reaction. She'd done it all too often herself.

The sheriff checked his watch. "I'll follow you back into town in case you pick up another nail in your tires. You probably should stay at the emergency displacement shelter at the school tonight. I'll head to your place first thing in the morning to check out the break-in damage and do my full report."

"I'll stay somewhere safe." The last thing she wanted was to cry herself to sleep with strangers around at the high school. Once she stopped moving, the wound of losing Crispin would crash over her. She blinked quickly and pressed her palm against the pocket where his necklace hid. "First, I need to head to my other horses at the film set's livery and check on them. They've been there since this morning. Not sure who last checked on them."

The sheriff crossed his arms, stubbornness brewing in his gaze until his radio crackled on his hip. "All right. Hold on, let's check your truck's gas tank. Lewis could have run out of gas along with the tire issues."

Sophie froze with her hand on the truck's handle. "Gas…"

The motorcycle man at her front door.

She spun back around to the sheriff. "What if it wasn't Lewis who broke into my house? He never admitted it exactly, and he claimed he was looking for his earbuds. I just assumed he was lying—"

"You caught the boy at your house. I know you and Marley are friends and you tried to help out, but we can't simply wish that people would do the right thing, or I'd be out of a job."

Sophie moved a pebble on the road with the toe of

her boot. "He still did plenty of wrong, but when I first arrived home this morning, there was a man at my house. I had hoped it was the bank department." She waved that thought away. "The man did take a while to turn around to greet me. Claimed he needed gas for his motorcycle. Even knew who Lewis was, calling him Lewy. What if the man broke into my house then? I hadn't gone inside to check before hurrying to the barn after he left. Perhaps Lewis tipped him off about something he thought was worth something? And Lewis stopped back by after the break-in; for what, I don't know yet. Maybe the lost earbud story was the truth."

She leaned her back against her driver's door. "The man could have been the person who stole Crispin's picture. Not Lewis."

Which was actually worse.

"So you're now thinking Lewis didn't steal anything from your house?" When had the sheriff gotten his notebook out?

Sophie combed her fingers through her pony-tailed hair. "I never actually saw anything on his person except the necklace. Not even the photo, and when I asked him, he claimed he hadn't taken any pictures. And hadn't broken in. What if Lewis had just been scared of getting caught again? Couldn't that have made him bolt?"

It probably would have made her flee. She'd begged her brother to move from Last Chance County because she was scared of all the rumors floating around about her.

The sheriff wrote in his notebook. "I won't rule it out yet. What did this motorcycle man look like?"

Sophie covered her face with her hands. That moment felt like years ago, but it had been less than twenty-four hours. "He had blue eyes. A spotty beard that was a mixture of gray and some white along with its reddish-brown." She pulled her hands away. "His hair was slicked back and brownish, and he wore a leather jacket with worn work boots. His Harley was older, and he had a gun half hidden on him."

The sheriff was no longer writing anything down. "Anything special about his voice?"

Sophie straightened. "A little raspy. Not sure that's the right word, but...you know who this man is, don't you?"

The sheriff held his notebook up toward his headlights and circled something. "I know that if it's him, he's wanted for other crimes."

"The other burglaries that have been happening around town?"

The sheriff only grunted and kept his attention on his notebook.

Something worse than burglaries then.

Sophie licked her lips. "If you can find him, I think I can ID him."

The sheriff snapped his notebook closed. "Sophie, if you see him again, you call me immediately. The more info I've gathered...We don't need that man angry at you. Especially if he thinks you know anything about what your brother could have been working on with Homeland Security."

He was right. This could turn into the car chase all over again. But this time, she didn't have her protector.

No, that wasn't right. She still had God.

"I understand. I won't go home tonight." She hopped in her truck and turned it on.

His radio listed a code of numbers and an address. The sheriff turned it down and pointed at Sophie. "I've got to answer this call out. You promise you'll go straight to the horses and back to the school?"

"After checking in at the livery, I'll probably go to Marley's instead of the school."

The sheriff hesitated.

"Sir, I've left my horses up at the set livery for over twelve hours. They could be without water."

His radio buzzed again. "Horses. Marley. Straight there and back. And if Lewis shows up, call me."

Sophie nodded and got into her truck. The sheriff raced to his car, turned on his lights, and sped away.

She drove with her hands gripped on the wheel. Her bright headlights did little to shine on the unknown thoughts racing through her head. The road snaked around, and finally the dusk to dawn light at the shadowed livery called to her in the darkness ahead.

She pulled up so her headlights hit the set's corral. They had left two of her horses outside the barn. That was not taking care of her animals. Good thing she'd returned to check on them.

Her taped ankle didn't slow her down as she headed for the corral. A solar-powered light shined down from the roof, casting an arrangement of eerie shadows on the film set's barn.

The air held only a hint of smoke that looked like clouds moving across the moonlight. Sophie ducked under the corral fence, and Thunderbolt stomped his foot. When she drew near, he twisted back his ears.

Sophie petted his head. "I'm so sorry. Your day hasn't exactly been smooth either."

The moon wasn't bright enough to see whether the corral's trough needed refilling. Her phone was still in the bag of rice drying out. So no flashlight.

Sophie stroked Goldie's nose first and then moved down the line, running her hand down their legs and inspecting them for any injuries. "We'll get you heading back inside for bed after I get you both some water and check on the others."

Goldie let out a sigh, as if she knew exactly what Sophie was talking about.

"Don't get too excited. You have to spend the night here."

Though as of right now, she at least had a house and barn to return to. Unless the fire changed direction for the third time. Or maybe it was the fourth?

She closed her eyes. Her ankle's throbbing had eased, but it ached with certain movements. As the entire day flashed bits and pieces through her mind, she glanced toward the western town set where she'd first thought she'd seen her brother. But even if someone was there, she couldn't tell in the darkness.

But all hope wasn't lost. Houston had prayed to find Frank. God had rescued them from the fire. He hadn't answered her pleas in the past how she'd hoped, but that didn't mean He wouldn't listen now. Marley had told her not to worry until she knew for sure.

Please let Crispin be alive. Somewhere. Somehow.

Thunderbolt pressed his head against her stomach.

"Thanks, bud." She rubbed under his ears.

Normally, this was why she'd rather be around animals than people. Animals got her. Or maybe she got them. Except being next to Houston had reminded her she was hiding from the fact that she was tired of being alone. And now with her one friend moving away...Was running a horse ranch by herself really what Sophie wanted?

After shutting the corral gate, she headed to the water spigot connected to a well just to the left of the fencing.

A stick snapped behind Sophie, and she glanced around.

Trees surrounded the barn and her. Her new, larger horse trailer was parked beside the barn where it had been blocked by a car earlier in the day. Thinking about that strange man at her house, and the break-in, had her on edge.

She didn't need to be caught out in the open. Plus, she needed more light. She jogged back toward her truck and flipped on her headlights to bright.

This time, when Thunderbolt stomped his foot and huffed, something caught her attention out of the corner of her eye along the tree line. Whether she could see it or not, something was in the woods. But was it human or animal?

She could get in her truck and drive away, but she wasn't about to leave her horses to face a mountain lion or some other predator. Yes, there was a man potentially looking for her, but it was more than likely an animal. One that viewed her animals as prey. She couldn't leave until she knew for sure.

Goldie twisted her ears to the right. Sophie's gaze

followed the tree line, and this time there was something.

Or rather someone.

This silhouette of a man wasn't the same build as the lanky teen or any of his friends. But he did have a hood pulled up to cover his head.

Sophie tightened her grip on the truck door. She was one second from hopping in and locking the doors. "What do you want?"

The man stepped into the truck's headlights. A baseball cap peeked out of the hoodie and stole her focus.

"Lamby?" The voice croaked as if he hadn't talked in days. Or perhaps he just hadn't said her name in...

Three long years.

A strangled sound hiccupped from her mouth. She knew that voice.

Crispin?

She took another step toward him.

But before she could get her brother's name out, someone else launched out of the woods. "Look out!"

The second man tackled Crispin from behind.

They both hit the dirt.

Sophie screamed.

Sometimes there wasn't time to think.

Houston's forearms took the brunt of the fall as both he and the man in the hoodie heading for Sophie slammed into the ground.

They landed outside the spotlight of Sophie's truck. The tall, dry grass scratched his cheek. The man squirmed beneath him. He'd been a head taller

125

than Houston. Broader shoulders too. But at least Houston had the surprise factor.

And surely, God would be on his side.

As Houston had been driving the curve toward the filming area, something reflected in his headlights in the woods. A bike, half hidden in a bush.

That was when the moonlight had snuck out from behind the clouds and highlighted a hooded figure watching Sophie with her horses.

The sound of Sophie's strangled yelp coursed through his mind. "Stop!"

Houston paused, and his grip loosened. Too much.

As quick as a fire could change directions, the man twisted his body in a way that Houston had only seen professional wrestlers perform. The man spun and aimed a gun at Houston's chest.

Houston only had time to swallow.

Sophie gasped and jumped in front of Houston. "Crispin. No!"

"Crispin?" The name released from Houston's tongue like a prayer. He hadn't taken his sights off of the man, whose gaze flicked to a spot behind Houston's shoulder.

Was there someone else hiding? But the guy's hesitation allowed Houston to step back in front of Sophie.

Crispin lowered the gun against his side but didn't hide it out of sight.

Sophie launched toward her brother. "Crispin! I knew you were alive."

Her brother wrapped Sophie up with the arm that wasn't holding the gun. "Course you did. I wrote to you."

"Until this year, and then the necklace—"

"I did write this year." Crispin's eyes narrowed on Houston. "Who is this guy? Can't be Landon. He's shorter."

Sophie backed up, wiping away her tears. Her shoulder brushed up against Houston, and he fisted his fingers to keep from tucking her against his side as Crispin had just gotten to do.

A half laugh, half cry came out of Sophie. "Of course it's not Landon. He got me fired from my dream job. And how did you even know who my ex was? That was only two years ago. Where have you been for all these years?"

"You're positive this is Crispin?" Houston said next to Sophie's ear, and the smell of coconut from her shampoo hit his nose. Only hours ago, she'd thought him dead. Houston couldn't recall running into her brother back in Last Chance County.

"You both need to stop saying my name." Crispin's voice filled with grit again.

Houston slipped his hand into Sophie's. She stepped closer to him. A person could change a lot in the amount of time Crispin had been gone. The hoodie covering a baseball hat shielded his face in the shadows of the night. It was hard to even get a read on his eyes that were constantly scanning the area.

"It's him." Sophie wiped her cheeks again with her free hand. "I thought you had been burned. Well, apparently, shot. Then burned."

Crispin tilted his head. For a moment it almost looked like there was scarring on the side of Crispin's neck, but it was hard to tell with his scraggly beard. "Wait. Homeland told you all that?"

"No, I knew after that first postcard arrived with the sunflowers and the story only you could know, that what they'd told me was a lie." She glanced at Houston and squeezed his hand. Then she lifted her quivering chin toward her brother. "I thought we found your body *today*."

"Today?" Crispin glanced over his shoulder. "Where was this?"

"We can get to all that." Houston moved his thumb over Sophie's hand. "But I think it's time for you to explain to your sister why you're here after years of disappearance." Houston pulled the main reason he'd driven out here over his head, Crispin's necklace that Sophie had left behind. "And why a teen found your necklace by a dead body."

Sophie sucked in a breath, and her hand slipped from Houston's. The lack of her touch made him want to lean closer to her, but he stood still.

She grabbed the necklace and pulled it into her chest. "How do you have this? I put it in my pocket."

Houston shoved his empty hands into his hotshot uniform. He didn't make time to change before he'd run to his truck. "It was left on the office chair."

She threaded her fingers through both rings. "And you came all the way out here."

Was that a statement or a question? If only she'd look at him now. Apparently, his ability to read high schoolers' tones didn't transfer over in this moment. Had he made the right move or not?

Probably tackling her brother hadn't helped.

Speaking of her brother, Houston lifted his brow toward Crispin. "Well?" Whatever was going on in Ember, it looked like Crispin was involved. Somehow.

The question he worried about the most was if Crispin's latest job would make Sophie some kind of target again.

"Do you trust this guy?" Crispin's voice pitched lower as he flicked his focus to Houston, then swept the area behind them, before finally circling back to Sophie. Who else did he think was lurking in the shadows?

Besides him.

"I'm right here. I can hear you."

Crispin only glared.

"I do trust him." Sophie brushed her arm against Houston's.

Houston squinted in the darkness. The man was stalling. Which was not a good sign. "I'm pretty sure this isn't about me."

"If you're connected to my sister in any way, I'm going to make it about you."

Sophie stepped in between Houston and Crispin. "We both can trust him. This is Houston James—"

"The guy from Last Chance County?" Crispin's eyes snapped to hers. "The one who stood you up, forbade you from visiting him in the hospital, and embarrassed you with all the rumors?"

Houston's arm went slack. "What rumors?"

Sophie avoided Houston's gaze. "It was a misunderstanding back then. We've worked out our history."

Sure, he'd apologized for the past, but apparently only for a part of it. "Soph, please, tell me. The rumors you faced were because of me?"

"Doesn't matter, Houston. It's in the past." Sophie's voice was quiet. Too quiet.

It was as if they were right back at the beginning of the day, with a wedge between them. Yes, he'd driven out here to make sure Sophie had her necklace. But he also wanted to what? Check on her.

Be brave enough to ask her out. To finally kiss her. Do the opposite of just allowing her to walk out of his life without seeing how she truly felt about him. Again.

Because Houston had always known that Sophie was something special. And he was smart enough to pray that she'd give him another chance. Or at least a real one.

Crispin shook his head. "Once you remained in the hospital, your friends spread awful things about her. For her sake alone, I'm not going to repeat any of those lies. But they made it clear that her worth was falsely inadequate, and they claimed their information had come directly from *you*. So really, you were the reason she wanted to leave Last Chance County."

"Stop, Crispin," she whispered. "I know now they weren't really his actual friends, and Houston's been with me every step of the disaster that was today. I trust him. The past or not." Her voice hitched at the end.

Houston's knees locked beneath him. The friends they had to be talking about were the two guys that had been over at the house the night of the house fire. "No, they weren't true friends. After the fire, they lied to the cops about even being at my house at all, let alone mentioning they'd lit a candle to light their joints while I must have passed out from the shots of whisky." Houston swallowed down the bitterness. "My poor choices hurt not only myself but also Sophie." And even worse, he did remember saying unkind things about her. Words he hadn't meant. Then or now. "Sophie, I'm so sorry."

One tear slid down her face until she turned away from him.

Her wound slammed into him harder than hitting the ground. "In my own stupid way, I'd been trying to protect you. That's not how it seems I know, but I'd seen how those guys had treated the girls they put on their next conquest list. They had started asking about you."

He raked his hand over his head and took a step back. "I'd been determined not to allow my lab partner—my friend—the girl that I..." Houston swallowed. "Determined not to find you on their list." He heaved out a sigh. "I finally explained to my brother that the house fire was my fault, and not his. How I had placed your note to meet me into Macon's locker instead to make it look like you wanted to meet him, all so Macon wouldn't be home when my supposed buddies came over. But I'd lied about how I hadn't liked you, Sophie." Oh, he had.

Houston squared his shoulders in front of Crispin. "But I knew your sister was too good for me, with all my angst and anger from my physical pain. I was a poor friend and thought sacrificing my relationship with her was the only way to get those guys to bring me their supposed healing in the forms of drugs and alcohol. I couldn't have been more wrong."

Crispin tsked. "Why are you still making up lies now? Those guys said you'd created those slurs before your house fire and burns. Don't you—"

"His nerve pain was from a failed bone marrow donation to his brother years before." Sophie's whisper cut through the night.

Houston hung his head. So many years of nerve pain, until God provided an experiment with electrotherapy that actually worked for him. But his agony didn't justify his hurtful actions. "I'm sorry,

Soph." He stepped toward Sophie, but Crispin slid in between. "I-I didn't want you to be treated like those other girls."

Except Houston had failed to protect her.

And worse, he'd been the one to hurt Sophie more.

NINE

SOMETIMES THE TRUTH HURT. YES, THOSE RUMORS had been awful. Supposedly meant only for his so-called buddies' ears to warn them away from her. She wished there was time to process through all of what Houston said about how he hadn't deserved her back then.

Sophie sniffed. "I forgive you, Houston."

He nodded.

But her words seemed to make him hunch his shoulders. There wasn't a moment more to spare on the past when the future kept knocking them over. So even if Houston had started the hurtful rumors, that wasn't the man he was now.

She turned toward Crispin. What she wasn't sure of was who her brother had become. There was something she couldn't quite read about him. She hated not even being able to trust those in her inner circle.

Plus, he'd yet to answer their questions.

When they'd hugged, he'd smelled different. Less like fruity cereal and peppermints and more of pine needles and smoke. His chest was broader. His beard had tickled her forehead. His compassion that used to extend off his tongue was replaced with harsh tones.

She fisted her fingers. "Please explain something about what happened to you, Crispin. Anything. I've missed you so much."

Crispin opened his arms and pulled her against his chest again. "Sorry, Lamby, that I was gruff earlier. You just have to stop saying my name so loud. I know it's always been your nickname for me...but it became my code name."

He picked up a long strand of her hair that had rested on her shoulder. "You grew out your hair again. Looks good."

That was one of the minor things on the detailed list the boys at Last Chance County had also made fun about. How her ponytail looked like horse hair. How only horses liked her. And other things that she'd blocked from her mind. "Does this mean you're finally done working for Homeland? Because you once told me that you'd never tell me your code name."

With a scowl, Crispin drew back. "There isn't time to explain everything."

"Why don't you start with the shot and burned dead body," Houston's voice held a stern quality she hadn't heard before. "The one your sister thought was *you*."

Crispin met Houston's glare with his own. "I'm sorry you thought it was me."

Sophie reached out her pinkie and touched Houston's clenched fist. "And the necklace?"

"It was stolen years ago. The man who pulled it off of me before an explosion—the one where I was reported dead—probably thought I had been killed. I guess he carried it as a trophy. Or maybe to show proof that he'd succeeded in his job of killing me." Crispin tucked his gun into his hoodie pocket. "Now, I assume he's the one who is dead, and I get to continue my mission."

Sophie opened up her palm. The rings balanced in the middle of the long chain. "He tried to kill you?"

Houston stepped closer to Sophie. "So you killed him instead?"

More a statement than a question, but Crispin simply narrowed his eyes. "Not the first time someone has tried to kill me, and I doubt it will be the last." He looked at Houston. "And no, I wasn't the one who killed him. Not that you're my keeper."

Sophie extended the necklace out to Crispin. "Who was he?"

He folded her fingers back around the rings and put his hand over hers. "You keep this. To remember them."

Sophie squeezed the rings into her palm. "You need to keep it. To remember to come home sooner to—"

"I never should have worn it in the field to begin with." Crispin gritted the words out.

Houston widened his stance. "Who was the dead body? The coroner has him now."

Crispin shook his head. "That's what I've been trying to find out."

Sophie dropped her hand away from her brother. He was allowing her to keep the necklace because he was leaving. Again. She knew it. There was something in his expression he wasn't saying. "So you really don't know. Or you just won't tell me?"

"Seems like something a federal agent could have

figured out in the *three* years he went missing," Houston said.

Crispin lifted the bill of his baseball cap. "If I had answers, I wouldn't have clearance to tell you. I've been cut off from my people. If I don't figure this out, there could be serious national security-level consequences. I tracked him down to this town."

Sophie heard what he wasn't saying. He hadn't come to Ember to see her. "It was you that I saw earlier at the film set, wasn't it? Why didn't you wait for me?"

"I couldn't let anyone connect us a second time."

An owl hooted in the distance. Then Goldie and Thunderbolt both nickered from the corral.

Sophie, Houston, and Crispin spun toward the sound.

Crispin put his hand on her shoulder. "We need to get out of the open. I know, Houston, that you weren't riding in Sophie's truck," Crispin murmured. "Where did you park?"

Houston tipped his head toward the woods that ran along the outskirts of the movie set. "My truck's back there on the road. I ran over because I thought you were the kid who stole Sophie's truck."

Did Houston think that was sufficient as an apology? Crispin seemed satisfied by it.

Men were odd creatures.

Crispin put his hands on his hips. "It was a mistake to contact you. I need to stay below the radar until this is over. For your sake and mine."

"Something we might agree on," Houston mumbled.

"I think we're both lucky my sister has a forgiving heart, or she wouldn't be giving either of us the time of day," Crispin said as he inspected the trees. "Lamby, can you still throw a punch like I taught you?"

"Like I'd ever forget where to place my thumbs ever again." Sophie walked toward the corral. "Let's get the horses loaded quickly. We'll talk about everything back at the house, which you can help me clean up."

Surely, she'd be safe if she wasn't the only one at her ranch. Especially since Crispin was trained and had a gun.

"No."

Sophie paused on her hurt ankle. She grunted and eyed her brother. "No what? I really don't want to leave my horses here when we can go—"

"I'm not bringing you any deeper into this mess. It's deep, Rachel. I mean, Sophie." He tugged on the hoodie's strings dangling against his chest. "I hate that you've had to already give up so much for the job that *I* chose. I don't know who I can completely trust. That's why it took three years to finally see you. I could never forgive myself if I led you to more danger."

Crispin shoved his hand into his hoodie pocket. "I wish you could have told me you moved up here. That's why you thought you didn't get a postcard this year. I didn't know you'd moved. You practically disappeared, untraceable through my normal channels. I sent it to your old address. I guess it didn't forward."

Sophie would have stumbled back if Houston hadn't steadied her. "What do you mean you didn't know I was up here? You were the one who set it up with the White family to have me inherit the land."

Houston raised his brow. "As in President White?"

She shrugged. "I have no clue which Whites. But that's the previous last name on the ranch."

Crispin ran his fingers along his beard. "Do you have any information on the inheritance, or who signed the paperwork?"

She shook her head. "Everything was done through a lawyer. You really didn't do this, or you don't want to tell me you know President White?"

Crispin's fingers paused and his jaw locked. "I've met the president. But I didn't give you a ranch. I never shared much about you. I also just always called you little lamb. I don't know how he found you and protected you for me."

His little lamb. That was what the man at her house had said.

She squared her shoulders. There would be another time to discuss that she owed her dream ranch to a stranger. Which was actually a lot more disturbing, but..."I think it's possible I might have met one of the Whites, or more than likely one of the people who might be after you."

"When?" Houston asked at the same time Crispin said, "You probably should have led with that information."

"Right." Sophie smacked her own forehead. "Makes perfect sense to not first hug my brother I thought was gone forever."

"When did you get this much sass?" Crispin gave Houston a deadpan expression. "Is this your doing?"

Houston held up his palms. "Is she safe? Someone broke into Sophie's house and stole a picture of you."

Her brother gave her a look, which if she were

young, would mean that she'd have to do all the dishes for the next week.

Sophie opened her mouth twice before words flowed. "I thought the break-in had been Lewis. My friend's nephew. He's been hanging out with the wrong kids. But then I started to think, what if it's more than just teens, like the creepy dude from this morning. What if he's the one who broke in and took your picture? Not Lewis."

"You have more of a description than creepy dude?" Crispin asked.

Sophie gave him everything she'd shared with the sheriff.

Crispin nodded. "I'll check him out, and if I give word then you've got to leave and change your name again. This time you send a postcard to our old California address and tell me you had a good time at the show or concert or something like that so I can know—"

"Wait. What? Go where?" She threw out her arms. "I have eight horses and a donkey." And hopefully more soon. Plus, she was finally starting to have a home again, even with her best friend leaving her. "I can't exactly pull up and stay at a hotel somewhere with all of them."

"You're more important than some animals."

"I can't abandon my horses." She knew what it felt like to feel so alone.

"Lamby, I know how much horses mean to you. Ever since that first counseling session after Mom and Dad...but these are bad guys. Not storybook ones. Or those cartoon ones you used to watch that would chase the sheep. Real ones. And I don't know who I can trust right now." He eyed Houston. "If I leave word, will you get her out of here if it comes to that?"

Sophie's ankle throbbed as she limped forward. "There's got to be another way. To stay safe and keep my horses."

No one else would love her horses like she did. No one loved her as much. She needed them as much as they needed her.

Crispin exhaled. "There's no time to be stubborn. I've got to keep you safe."

She blinked at her brother. Demanding and unyielding was not the kind of protection she wanted.

"I know where she can go." Houston's expression pulled tight. "To be safe."

She wasn't going to like her brother and Houston working together.

"I'm not going to run." Sophie stepped back from both of them. No, she was tired of doing that. Failed at doing that. Ran from the earthquake. From Last Chance County. From being fired at the horseracing farm. Scared or not, she was going to do what she always did.

Face what came at her, alone.

"Where would she go?"

He'd gotten Crispin's attention, but Houston wasn't about to give up that information.

Crispin's baggy hoodie and cargo pants didn't give too much away, but probably he weighed a bit more than Houston. Which meant Houston couldn't toss Crispin far. And Houston trusted the guy even less than he could throw him.

It looked like he and Sophie were finally on the same page over needing to be cautious about her brother. Crispin didn't realize how important her horses were to her. They were like her family, because she hadn't really had anyone for her.

"Someplace no one could trace her and her horses," Houston offered.

Crispin gave a brief half smirk. "If you two are together, they'll track her there."

"Please stop talking as if I'm not right here. I'm not a kid to be dumped on someone else."

"It wouldn't be dumping at all." Houston didn't want her to think of it that way.

"Right. I'm sure your sister-in-law's family wouldn't think you showing up with me to bunk with them would be odd. And who says I even want to go back to Last Chance County? I'm not giving up my life again."

He barely refrained from smacking his forehead. He didn't exactly want her brother knowing anything else. "Never said where it was."

Sophie's eyebrows rose, and she propped her fists onto her hips. "You learned to ride with your sister-in-law's family's horses, right?"

"He was trying to keep the information from me." Crispin leaned toward him. "Do you really think I'd stay away for so long to protect her, only to let her get hurt now?"

"No offense. But I don't exactly trust you."

"Fair enough." Crispin nodded. "But we want the same thing."

"Stop doing that guy stare down stuff." Sophie sighed. "I'll make my *own* choice about where I go and when." Sophie held up one finger toward her brother.

"I have a condition. You find a way to stay in contact better. That's number one." She held up another finger and limped forward.

Houston frowned. Was her ankle hurt worse than she admitted back at HQ?

"And number two," she raised another finger and shifted on her feet. "You're going to ask me to do whatever favor you're wrestling over inside your head."

Crispin's gaze dropped to Sophie's feet. "Is your foot hurt?"

"Don't *even* with another whole changing the subject."

Crispin grunted. "It was an honest question, and I'll figure out another way for what I need. I don't want your help if it puts you in danger, Lamby."

"So there is something you need," Houston said.

"We can figure it out together, right here, or at my house." Sophie didn't back down. "Now, what is it?"

For the first time, Crispin seemed to wilt. Bad guys and national security didn't bother him. But when his sister stood up for herself, he melted. The guy leaned his back up against the truck. "I have to get a message to someone I used to know."

Sophie wrinkled her nose. "Are we talking a package or a phone call type of message?"

He pulled out a flip phone from his pocket. Even in the darkness, the cracked plastic was obvious. "I need to charge this."

Houston tugged his phone out of his pocket. "Here."

Crispin shook his head. "Traceable."

"Then we'll get another burner," Sophie suggested. "An unregistered phone."

Crispin checked the horses in the corral. "My old partner thinks I'm dead, and it needs to stay that way. For his sake. But he still needs to know the brothers are back. That's why I need you to contact him and tell him that. 'The brothers are here.' He'll know what it means."

Houston frowned. "How do we know if we have the right guy, if we're just calling numbers on your list?"

"He goes by Samuel Mudd."

Sophie opened up her passenger-side door and plugged it into her charger with the cigarette lighter. She opened her glove box and found a blue folded piece of paper. She unfolded it and held out three twenties to her brother. "Here. It's not much. But I have a bit more in my…"

Crispin pulled her into another hug. "This isn't forever."

Sophie turned. "Let's get the horses loaded. I'll hook up the trailer first."

"I'll help you line up the hitches."

Houston went to leave, but Crispin's hand clamped down on his shoulder. "I'm trusting you to keep her safe."

Houston nodded. "I got this."

He must have uttered the magical words because Crispin let him go. The horse trailer was connected to the truck, and then Houston and Crispin helped load the horses from the barn.

Crispin led a gray horse by a purple lead rope and hooked his thumb over his shoulder. "The last horse only has a halter on."

"I can handle it."

A scream from outside the barn pierced through Houston's heart. "Sophie!"

He sprinted past Crispin and arrived outside first.

Sophie was on the ground, holding her head in her palms at the end of her trailer.

"What happened?" Houston dropped before her.

Crispin slid in behind him. "Are you—"

"He rammed me over and took Goldie and your phone. I should have paid more attention to her snicker earlier. She had been trying to tell me someone was there."

"Who?" Houston's breath caught in his throat.

"Where did he go?" Crispin ordered.

"They galloped that way." She pointed toward the back of the barn that butted up against the woods. "We've got to go get the phone." She pushed herself up but wobbled.

Houston wrapped his arms around her shoulders. And saw the blood pooled on the side of her head. "I'm taking you to the hospital."

She shook her head, but then moaned. She leaned against Houston's chest. "We have to help Crispin."

"No. This is my problem. I'll deal with it." Crispin locked eyes with Houston. "Remember what I told you."

Houston tightened his hold on Sophie. He had no other plans except protecting the woman he had never stopped loving.

TEN

"SOPHIE LAMB."

The voice held more of a whine than concern. And even worse, the voice wasn't deep. It wasn't Houston who had been sitting beside her hospital bed holding her hand.

The starched bed sheets chafed against her skin. Sophie squinted her eyes open, and a whimper might have graced her lips. It was no nurse with discharge papers. Rather, the nosy Betty Adams.

The clock on the wall ticked past one in the morning. Apparently, gossip research didn't have a bedtime.

Betty shook Sophie's shoulders harder. The woman's manicured nails poked Sophie as Betty's bracelets rattled more than Sophie's throbbing head. "Sophie, dearest, you've got to wake up."

Sophie moved her neck to the right. Her wound above her ear scratched against the pillow behind her head. This time she did groan.

The curtain that had been around Sophie's bed swung open. Marley held a steaming cup of what was more than likely coffee with one generous spoon of sugar. Her brows tugged low. "Betty," Sophie's best friend stage whispered. "What are you doing? Sophie and the entire hospital floor need to rest."

Betty straightened her name badge on her bright red sweater. "The hospital strives to have a five-star customer satisfaction. One of my many volunteer tasks is to make sure everyone is getting the extra care they require."

Apparently, care didn't mean sleep. Sophie squeezed her eyes shut again. Couldn't she be nosy and quiet? "I'll hand out five stars when they let me go. How much longer will the paperwork take?"

"Let me check. In the meantime, I'll bring you some water and ice chips while you wait, dear."

Sophie shook her head but stopped. Her head didn't hurt if she didn't move. Or really think.

Marley gripped the cup with both hands as if she forced herself to hold something, or she might wring a certain someone's neck. "That is...kind of you, Betty," she said through her teeth. "But Sophie doesn't need water or ice chips. Not even cookie dough ice cream. She needs rest."

Betty turned to Sophie and patted her hand. The hand that, an hour or so earlier, Houston had held while Sophie received five stitches in the back of her head. "Ice chips will help you stay awake. After a concussion, you're not supposed to sleep. Everyone should know that." She sent a side eye toward Marley. "We can't have you forgetting every detail of what caused your accident."

Marley exhaled and made the steam from her mug blow Betty's way. "And how do you know that Sophie might have a concussion?"

A sheepish expression crossed Betty's face. "It's my job to understand the patient's needs."

Marley opened her mouth, but Sophie rushed out her own reply. "No concussion." The quicker Betty got some of the specifics she craved, the sooner she could rest. "They thought so at first but ruled it out. The doctor didn't say anything about not sleeping. Thankfully, because it's way past my bedtime." Was Houston asleep in the hallway somewhere?

Sophie detangled the sheet that had been resting over her legs. She didn't want to look too comfy here, or they might just allow her to stay. And that wasn't happening. "Thank you for your volunteer work."

Betty blushed. "I strive to always be helpful."

That's not exactly how Sophie would have worded it. She kept her attention locked on Betty and not her friend, who was more than likely rolling her eyes.

Betty waved a goodbye to Sophie, but stopped as she closed the curtain behind her. "Oh, and I heard that a horse was found wandering down one of the county roads. You're missing one, right? The Johnsons are caring for it until you can come pick it up. Thought you'd want to know."

For once, Betty's nose for gossip was useful. "Yes, I'll rest better knowing my horse is safe. Thank you, Betty." That info was better than any ice chips or ice cream. Goldie was okay, but what about Crispin and his phone?

After the curtain closed, Marley slumped down on the edge of Sophie's bed. "She's trying to help all right. Help find herself more gossip. Sorry I wasn't in here when she snuck in. She cornered Houston earlier, asking him an entire game show worth of questions. The man had *help me* written on his face, and he looked as tired as you do right now.

Sophie fluffed the pillow that had gone flat behind her. "So, Houston's getting a coffee?"

Did Houston even drink coffee? Their time together today hadn't been filled with small get-to-know-you-again questions, but rather with real life responses that displayed the true character of someone that often takes months to uncover. Plus the truth about their high school past.

Marley took a sip and wiped her lip. "No, he left."

Sophie stared past her friend at the mint green curtain. Houston was gone. Of course he was. It was late, and he needed to rest. And there was no real reason for him to stay.

Sophie twisted the edge of the sheet in her grip. No reason except her.

He hadn't even said goodbye.

Marley scooted more onto the bed, bumping her knee into Sophie's foot. "I was right."

Sophie reached back and touched the tender spot above her ear. Her finger pricked the end of one of the pointed stitches, and she jerked her hand away. The first and only other time she'd received stitches, no one had held her hand. When she'd been taken by ambulance after the earthquake, her brother had been stuck across town. He wasn't there for the car accident either.

Sophie sat up. "If you were right about leaving soon, I'm afraid you can't trade in your best friend card yet. I need to bum a night's sleep at your house for whatever's left of the morning. That is if they ever let me out of here. And did Lewis ever make it home?"

Marley set her cup down on a side table next to the bed. "No. And I'm beyond worried. But this isn't the first time he's disappeared for this long. Thank you for worrying about him, but no, I was right that Houston is cute, even for not being my preferred blond, and no, I'm not going anywhere."

Sophie raised her brows.

Marley waved a finger at her. "Okay. Yes, I'm moving. But not today, and I'm not disappearing from your life completely. I'll still only be a phone call away."

Until she got too busy with her new happily-ever-after life, far from Sophie.

"Speaking of phones…"

Sophie's heart thumped as Marley pulled something out of her purse.

Could Marley have gotten Crispin's phone somehow?

But Marley only extended a piece of paper. "I told Houston to head home and get some sleep. He was stubborn, but the man was beyond exhausted, and he has to go back to work tomorrow. You wouldn't have wanted him here if you had seen him. I think it helped that you had fallen asleep. That was, until Betty." She jiggled the piece of paper. "He left his number."

Sophie took the number. The area code was from Last Chance County. "My phone's in my truck, and I'm not even sure it still works."

Marley grabbed her coffee. "Right. I get it. It's not like you can get another phone or anything and call Houston later."

Not the one Crispin had, no, but that wasn't what Marley was talking about. Sophie turned and dangled her feet over the side of the bed. "It was good to reconnect with Houston. But maybe that's all we needed. To heal the past."

Marley nodded. "Of course. Why put him in your future when he's already been in the past?"

"See, you get it."

Marley fluttered her free hand in front of her face. "Sophie, no. Maybe Houston's not the one to partner beside you and challenge you to be the best version of yourself. To encourage your dreams and yet keep your feet planted when you get off track. But, maybe the man who would have held your hand all night while you slept, or survived a fire with you, might be worth a second look."

Oh, Houston was worth it. But Sophie simply lifted one shoulder. "Not sure the timing will work. He's got plans outside of Ember. And I want to build more barns here. I'm a horse mom. I have to be practical."

Marley adjusted the purple headband holding back her curls. "I hear you; I really do. All the logistics that I thought of when Brady and I started dating online. But what I'm not sure of is...what you're actually afraid of."

Afraid of? Sophie swallowed. "Today, or rather yesterday, was pretty awful." And yet, her time with Houston had made her smile.

Marley put her hand on Sophie's arm. "I think you know exactly what I mean, and you keep hiding from it. You've shared enough of your past and your different moves. Don't hate me, but Sophie, you're a runner. Sometimes the good things in life are scary at first. God wants you to seek Him when you're fearful, not hide from Him. Sometimes the bravest thing to do is simply trust Him."

Sophie tightened her fingers around the end of the sheet and balled it into her palm. She didn't always run from her problems, did she? And, sometimes, it was God who she was fearful of. Sometimes it didn't always feel like He was on her side, not with so many loved ones He'd taken from her. She opened her mouth, but a nurse with puppies on her scrubs walked around the curtain with a smile.

She held up a set of papers in her hands. "Looks like you're free."

Sophie pushed herself off the bed. She breathed through the tender pain on the side of her head. Yes, she was free from the hospital. But her answer to her friend's question kept hold of her mind.

One of Sophie's fears was losing more people she cared for. She'd already lost so many. What if she let herself completely fall for Houston again? It wasn't like he had a safe job. Could her heart stand letting go of someone else?

Houston's phone burned a hole in his pocket. Not literally. Thankfully, the hotspots they'd patrolled in the direction of Sophie's ranch surrendered without much of a fight. But the fire had headed east instead, which was both a blessing and a curse. And even with his fire ax in his grip, securing the latest fire line, his hands itched to check to see if Sophie had called him.

In over nineteen hours, she hadn't.

Houston sent the sharpened Pulaski into the ground, widening the trench. The sunset peppered through the hazy air twenty miles from Sophie's ranch. Houston should have gotten at least five hours of sleep to help with today's work. Should have, but didn't. Too much of last night had plagued him. Sophie's anguish. Her willingness to forgive him. Her physical pain.

Houston rested his Pulaski over his shoulder and wiped the sweat from his forehead. *Please Lord, let her heal quickly.*

Orion marched toward the right, probably checking Houston's work, while Charlie walked up on Houston's left.

As he eyed Houston, Charlie took a long pull from his water bottle. "Did you run out of water?"

Houston tugged out his water bottle and shook it before taking a drink. "No rookie mistakes to admit to today."

And hopefully, there wouldn't be any.

Charlie frowned. "Except maybe a good night's sleep. You look exhausted. I wouldn't have had you out on this assignment at all."

Houston popped his water lid back down. "Fire doesn't wait for anyone. Tired or not."

"Exactly."

Houston locked his gaze on the man who wasn't usually full of sharp comebacks. At least not ones directed at Houston.

But before Houston could say something his tired tongue might regret, Charlie sighed. "It was weird not having you playing your guitar last night at the barracks."

Houston huffed. "Even I wouldn't enjoy a song after one in the morning when I got in."

Charlie adjusted his backpack straps around his shoulders. "Nah, probably not. But it felt odd without the normal *It Is Well* hymn you strum nightly. The crew needed the comfort when you were still missing. Logan had to play it on his phone."

The song was Houston's favorite old hymn since one of the nurses in the burn unit at the hospital whistled it so often that Houston had asked her what she was singing. The song hadn't been familiar to him then, but after God had redeemed his life, it had become his anthem. One he too often sang without truly reflecting on the lyrics. Until the wildfire with Sophie.

Charlie kicked at a stick on the ground. "We didn't go to bed until we heard you were okay. But if I was the chief, I would have let you sleep in this morning."

Was that supposed to be comforting? "Yeah, well, I got some big shoes to fill out here."

"Or maybe you need to put on your *own* boots. I'm not your brother, but Macon was my old chief." Charlie crossed his arms. "I know he wasn't happy with you coming out here."

"That's one way to put it." Houston arched his toes in his newer pair of boots. "He said I didn't need to line myself up for failure."

After a pause, Charlie said, "Don't think he meant it as it sounds."

"Not sure there's another way to hear that."

Charlie raised his palm. "I also know that you and your brother are a bit stubborn, and you're out here to prove yourself. Which is both encouraging and a bit frightening as your teammate."

Houston wiped sweat off of the burn scars on the back of his neck. "I might be frightening to look at, but I'm not going to freeze up and put you or the other guys in danger."

Not again.

"I didn't mean frightening in either of those ways. It wasn't fair what happened to you back at Last Chance County Church. Eli didn't have the experience you had with those kids. If I was still in town, I'd give them a piece of my mind."

Why wouldn't news travel here? Houston closed his eyes. "Eli called me last night."

"Please don't tell me that he's quitting and you're leaving us."

"Not exactly. It looks like I might have an opportunity to stay longer in Ember. I didn't get into Truth Seminary. I'd planned to maybe attend another one somewhere else, but last night, while I was at the hospital with Sophie, I ran across an elder from Ember First Church. He said that the church had several open positions. Asked me to think about applying."

"You're the guitar playing hotshot, right? Heard you humming when I came in." The white-haired doctor that had checked on Sophie while she was sleeping asked.

Houston offered his free hand. The one not tucked around Sophie's lying on the hospital bed. "I normally just go by Houston James."

The man chuckled. "While you're here in Ember, our praise band could use some new members."

"I've only ever led youth in worship before. Well, and whatever you call playing at our dorms at night. But I thought of that more as a witnessing opportunity."

"Youth, huh?" The man raised his white brows. "Did you ever happen to teach too?"

Houston traced his thumb along Sophie's smooth hand. She made a soft sigh. "Used to."

"Bet you still can. Say, our church has several open positions, why don't you come on down and—"

"You probably don't want me."

The man tilted his head. *"That sounds an awful lot like something Moses might say."*

Houston grimaced. He wished he could say he'd been like Moses. Been given a great task. *"My story is more like Joseph's."*

The doctor nodded. *"Been molding you through trials, has He? I've had a few past events not go as planned for my life too."* He kept moving his head up and down, slow and steady, as if counting through each memory. *"I've proved to be a stubborn listener, but looking back, those trials or dreaded circumstances—or in your firefighter world, an ignited flashover, hot and heated one moment—God used those to make me into the man He wanted for His plans."*

He tugged on his white doctor's jacket. *"I wanted to be a pilot, but my vision at the time was no good. It took me a while to realize why I needed to be a doctor instead."* He winked. *"Trust me, God always knows best. Take some time. Pray. Come visit the church and see what happens after that."*

His plans. The words had repeated inside of Houston's mind all day, behind the backdrop of digging and mopping up.

Now, Charlie's smirking face erased the memory of the doctor's thirty-year age difference. "I figured you might be changing your mind about staying in town." He ran his knuckles over the five-o'clock shadow along his chin. "I guessed there might be another reason why you might want to stay near Ember. You looked a little cozy with Sophie after the smokejumpers picked you both up on the town's gossip page. Working at a local church here, not sure why you hadn't looked into that before now."

Houston crossed his arms over his chest. Because he'd set his mind on his own plans. "Even if I did stay past the hotshot season, it couldn't be just for Sophie."

Charlie grunted. "You'd think that since you've worked at a church, you wouldn't lie as much."

"I'm not sinless...and I'm not lying."

"If you're worried about her not liking you, the crew took a poll, and we think she likes you back."

Houston raced his hands over his bald head. "I haven't had the best experience with women since all this." He pulled his collar away from his scars. "Once had a woman leave the moment she'd met me in person after we'd supposedly dated online for four months."

"Anyone who looks at you and sees anything other than a dedicated, honorable man...sounds like she wasn't the right one for you."

Orion jogged toward them, his pack thumping against his back. He checked his watch and pulled out his own water jug. "Good work. The fire trench is spot on. The fire doesn't look like it will be an issue tonight. The Trouble Boys are almost here to replace us." Orion squinted away from the sunset and then pointed back toward the unburned trees. "Yep. There they are. Perfect. James, if I were you, I'd call it a night early. Both you and Benning can head to the buggy."

As Charlie and Houston walked back, Houston pulled out his phone. Not a single missed call notification; however, there was the symbol of a new voicemail.

His fingers fumbled over the phone until he clicked the first voice message. It was the pastor at Ember Community Church, wanting to set up a time to meet and discuss things. Houston didn't know what God would do there, but this time there wasn't a sense of dread for the unknown. Maybe Houston had zeroed in on too much of what he'd wanted out of his future without leaving any room for God to have His say.

Houston saved the first message, and then Sophie's voice brought his feet to a halt.

She'd called.

"Hey, Houston." Her voice was soft, hesitant. "Sorry to bother you. I'm not sure if you're working or..."

Bother him? He'd been looking forward to hearing from her. Seeing how she was feeling.

"...I don't know who else to call. I probably should contact the sheriff, but it involves Crispin, well, his phone, and..." Her heavy sigh made Houston squeeze his phone to his ear.

"My phone stopped working. From too much water. But you kind of already know that story. Anyway, when I got a new one, I had a voicemail from Lewis. He has Crispin's phone. He was the one who took Goldie and knocked me over. He said he didn't mean to hurt me..."

The Trouble Boys were right in front of Houston, and he waved and hiked after Charlie.

"He wants to give the phone back. He sounded...a little scared. But he's not answering my calls. His message said to park where the old one-room school used to be. I have to be there at eight tonight. And I have no way to get hold of Crispin."

Houston had almost caught up to Charlie when Sophie's words hit his chest. Hard.

"And I'd really like it if you were there with me."

There was no other place Houston wanted to be, except beside Sophie.

The message ended and Houston checked the time. Only ten minutes to get there. He wanted to call Sophie to let her know he would be there, but she didn't leave her number. His phone must have been out of service when she'd called, and therefore it only registered her voicemail and not her number.

Charlie turned and took his own phone away from his ear. "Most of the smokejumpers and a few of our hotshots are eating at Hotline Saloon. I know you're probably heading to bed early, but you at least want to grab a to-go meal?"

Houston shook his head. He wouldn't be heading anywhere except toward Sophie. "I've got somewhere else to be."

He prayed he'd get there in time.

ELEVEN

WHETHER SOPHIE WAS A FOOL OR NOT WAS STILL up for debate. She checked the time. Fifteen minutes after eight. The sparse gravel drive that led up to what was left of the one-room schoolhouse was empty. Well, except for Sophie inside of her truck. She hadn't called Marley because she didn't want to get her hopes up until she'd seen Lewis.

But it looked like the teen ghosted Sophie.

The tree line behind the school stood like a darkened army, guarding the woods. But there almost looked like a path between the trees on the left-hand side. If this were a movie, she would be yelling at the character to not even think about going into the woods.

But Sophie needed that phone. She needed to call the person her brother had to get a message to. The sooner that threat was finished, the sooner her brother could return to her.

The wind rustled the branches above, and her heartbeat rang like a gong in the quiet night.

Wait. Was that a light ahead? Maybe Lewis was here as he said.

She got out of her truck and walked to the edge of the pathway into the woods. Her ankle no longer ached as it was safely nestled inside of her ankle support brace. She squinted into the rows of trees. Yes, there was a light. But was it getting closer or farther away?

She checked her phone. No response from Houston. He wasn't coming. She had to face another battle by herself.

Well, not really alone. God was with her, and Marley had been right. She did tend to run. To hide from her problems. But she needed to stop fearing God in the wrong ways. He wasn't out to cause her harm, even when things didn't go her way. She needed to be brave and trust Him fully.

She dialed Marley, but it went to voicemail. "Hey, I just wanted to let you know Lewis left a message for me to meet him at the old one-room school. I probably should have told you sooner, but I didn't want to get your hopes up about his location. I see a light in the woods. He must have a hideout out there or something, so I'm going to go find him."

And get her brother's phone.

After ending the message, she crept along the path, weaving in and out of the trees. She used her flashlight app to light her way. "Lewis?"

A faint voice had her feet entering the path. By the time she was deep enough to no longer see the outline of her truck behind her, the light she'd spotted from the driveway had split into two. Then four. Or rather the lights became a group of lit tiki torches spaced around a building that was more a metal lean-to. A blue tarp, which was fastened to the front of the building, flapped in the wind. There were two piles of dirt in the center of the lit area. But there were still plenty of low-hanging branches near the tiki torches.

Apparently, Lewis wanted another forest fire.

She rested her palm on a tree whose trunk was as wide as Sophie was tall, and something seemed to stop her from calling out to Lewis.

At the sound of a hearty laugh, Sophie shut off her flashlight. She tucked herself behind the tree. Squatting down, she peered around the rough bark.

Someone grunted. "How much longer do I got to dig?" A younger male voice wailed. A teen's head popped up from out of a hole beside one of the piles of dirt. "And why aren't you digging, Finn?"

If Finn was there, then the first one was probably Preston. The kids Houston said he'd found setting off firecrackers with no regard for the wildfire and Lewis's so-called friends.

Finn walked out from behind the tarp, pulling something behind him on the ground. "Because someone's got to watch Lewis before he runs off again."

Lewis was the squirming something being pulled on the ground. Not only were his feet tied together, but also his hands.

Finn released him, and Lewis sat up. His shirt was stained with grime, and if the light wasn't playing tricks on her, a darkening bruise decorated his cheek. "I didn't run off." Lewis's tone was gruffer than she'd ever heard. "I got info that can get us money. You gotta believe me."

Sophie froze with her hand on a branch.

The phone. Or maybe even her too? Had Lewis called her, knowing she'd come and be spotted?

She heard someone snort. "As if you know anything. You're why Ozzy hasn't paid us anymore."

Then Preston's head popped up from behind the pile of dirt. He wiped his forehead. "At least get Lewy in here and let him dig instead of me."

Lewy. The motorcycle man had called Lewis that as well.

It was all coming together. Motorcycle guy, probably named Ozzy, was these kids' boss or leader —mentor—that's what the man had said at her ranch.

She pulled up the sheriff's personal number he'd given her after he'd stopped by her house, then sent him a message to hurry out to her location.

"You're wasting your time." Lewis pushed himself up, but his feet tangled together, and he tripped. "If another cave entrance was here, you'd have already found it." He snarled from his position on the ground.

Finn marched over. He picked Lewis up by his shirt, only to shove the smaller teen back down. "Not another word until Ozzy arrives. He'll decide what to do with you for going off without us."

Lewis opened his mouth, but Finn drew out a gun from his pocket.

Sophie pressed her fingers into the tree bark. She needed to get out of there. She didn't trust Finn without a gun, much less with one. But what about Lewis?

Lord, please send help, quick.

With his other hand, Finn pulled out a knife. "Pretty sure Preston would love to stop digging and hold you down while I cut out your tongue."

Preston flung out a shovel full of dirt, which thudded against Lewis's back. "Better than being over here doing. All. The. Digging." With a grunt, he climbed out of the pit and threw the shovel down at Lewis's feet. "Get in there before Finn does what he says."

As they untied his hands, Lewis obeyed his so-called friends. Sophie leaned farther around the tree. How was she going to help? Lewis had made his choices, and Crispin could deal with his national security threat. She was hardly qualified to help with that. Her past good deeds hadn't exactly been giving her blessings lately. But still, she couldn't leave the kid.

When she turned to check on Lewis, a hand covered her mouth.

Sophie thrashed, but an arm circled around her. She twisted. Thrashed some more. But the arms only held on tighter.

"It's me," the voice whispered beside her ear.

Houston.

She stilled. He'd come. But knowing that he'd snuck up on her didn't exactly bode well.

She relaxed her shoulders, and he released her.

He kept his head near hers and whispered, "Sorry I'm late, and by the way, you are never a bother."

She leaned into the man she'd come to depend on. She had been right to call him.

Houston pulled back, and even in the moonlight, his eyes seemed to say more than his words. His hand drifted down her arm, and then he laced his fingers through hers. He peeked around the tree and then tugged on her hand, leading them back toward the school.

She crept after him as they weaved around the path, keeping a tree between them and the lit area.

Sophie squeezed Houston's fingers, tugged him

behind another enormous tree trunk. "We have got to save Lewis. They have him tied up. They kept talking about someone else coming. And we need to get Crispin's phone back. If it can lead someone to my brother in any way—"

"They also have a gun, Sophie. Teens or not, I can't win against bullets." Houston pressed his back against the tree and yanked out his phone. He touched a few things on the screen and then placed the phone by his ear and whispered, "Sheriff? It's Houston and Sophie. We have Lewis in sight, but we can't get to him because his buddies have a gun."

Sophie's heartbeat thundered louder in her ears than Houston's soft tone. She watched the boys from around the tree. Finn remained watching Lewis while Preston took a drink from a can. Neither of them looked like they could hear Houston.

Except...was that another light? Had Ozzy already arrived?

She inched toward them, but as she did, a branch she hadn't seen whacked against the stitches on her head. A groan rushed from her mouth. She bit down on her lip and jumped back behind the tree.

Houston's arms wrapped around her. "You okay? I knew I shouldn't have left you at the hospital. Did you have a concussion after all?"

"I'm fine."

"Soph." She didn't have to look at Houston to hear the plea in his murmur.

"I just scraped my stitches."

She heard Houston swallow. His arms tightened around her. His head lowered toward hers. "I hate that you're hurt. I—"

The sound of someone spitting made Sophie whip her head around, making the side of her head ache.

"Interesting to find you out here. Little far from home, aren't we?" Not one of the boys, but a familiar voice. "Why don't you head toward the camp?"

His evil tone shuddered through her, and Houston tugged her even closer to his chest.

The man stepped into the moonlight, and the gun in his hand shined as bright as the tiki torches. He aimed it at Houston, then Sophie. "I'll get to thank you proper for that gas you provided and for the intel inside your house." The man who had been at her ranch just a day ago raised his gun. "Move slowly, Romeo. Or first I'll shoot your Juliet. Then I'll kill you. Slowly."

Why did Sophie keep putting the man she'd fallen for in danger?

Houston knew he needed God's help in keeping Sophie alive. The man held his gun steady like he'd done this before. More than likely, the gunman wasn't going to ever let them go. They'd seen his face.

Sophie inched her chin closer to Houston's. "If you—" Her words were only a breath, but the man, behind them, tsked.

"I've got a clean shot, Ms. Lamb. I think I'm being mighty nice by reminding you to withhold from speaking to Romeo, or I'll make you watch him die instead of letting you have the easier death."

She shuddered against him. Houston gripped her hand tighter.

Lightly, she loosened her hold, and she moved her thumb until it was pressed by his palm. She drew a circle with her thumbnail. Then over again. He glanced down at her, but she kept her face forward as they walked in front of the gunman.

Her fingers repeated the exact motion again.

It almost felt like she was tracing a letter. Wait. Of course, she was writing letters against his skin.

He tapped his thumb against her hand to let her know he understood.

Her thumb danced again. The first letter was 'I'.

Then an 'F'.

As they marched closer to the two lit tiki torches, Houston's foot hit a stick. The snap echoed through the woods as Sophie had finished tracing the letter 'Y'.

Finn charged toward the edge of the cleared, lit space. "Who's there? Is that you, Ozzy?"

"Boy," Ozzy gritted out from behind Houston. "You've done missed the opportunity to ask that question. You never let anyone sneak up on you. And I don't like to be awakened from my nap, so your news better be about how you found that cave entrance. You won't like the outcome if you boys keep failing me."

Preston scooped up a handful of dirt and flung it at Lewis down in a hole. "As always, it was Lewy's fault, Ozzy. He's the one who makes us look bad to your cousin."

From inside the pit, Lewis's eyes widened for a second. Houston stepped into the light with Sophie at his side. Sweat dripped from the boy's forehead. One of his wrists had a rag tied on it, and his hands were tightened around a shovel. He didn't say a word in defense, only dropped his gaze to the dirt piled around him.

Ozzy kept his gun pointed at Sophie and Houston as he walked toward the pit. "Did you find it yet?"

"Won't be long, Oz." Finn flipped his wrist, sending his blade out and then pushing it back in with his thumb. He then pulled out his gun from his back pocket. "Please tell me I get to use this finally?"

Ozzy grunted. He pointed his gun at the ground beside Preston. "Ms. Lamb. Get on your hands and knees. Romeo get beside Finn over there. Let's find out what you know."

"We don't know anything. Just let us go," Houston said.

Sophie didn't drop her hand from his. Neither did Houston.

He just needed a second for a plan. Or rather, another miracle.

Lord, we need another Red Sea moment. I'm trusting in Your plan.

A gunshot cracked through the night.

Sophie squealed and pressed her head against him. Houston's breath evaporated. He hadn't been shot, but had she?

His hands went to her shoulders, to her chin, only to see her eyes staring at him with the fear that coursed through him.

"If I wanted to shoot you, I would have," Ozzy spat. "Wow, I'm being an awfully patient man. Get over by Finn, or the next time I won't be aiming at the sky."

Sophie released her hold, and Houston inched away.

Finn leaned over. His breath smelled like sweat

and alcohol. "I'm pretty sure I'm about to have more fun than yesterday's squirrels."

Ozzy motioned to Lewis, and he threw the shovel out of the pit toward Houston's side and scrabbled out.

"Did you lead these two out here?"

Lewis's gaze darted toward Sophie.

Finn kicked some dirt at Lewis. "Course he did. He can't do nothing right."

Except Lewis had been the one to run for the four-wheeler when Finn was in Orion's grasp, but Houston pressed his lips together.

Ozzy turned his gun around and held it out toward Lewis. "Then you fix the problem. Show me you can handle this life. Shoot Romeo first."

"No, Lewis!" Sophie pushed herself up, but Preston grabbed her by her ponytail.

Ozzy swung his gun around and was in the middle of aiming it at Sophie when Lewis said, "I got some information that your cousin is gonna like. Enough to pay all of us."

Ozzy scratched the side of his temple with the butt of the pistol. "Spit it out, then."

Lewis wiped his forehead. "I think I found information on one of the guys the brothers want."

Ozzy ran his tongue over his teeth. "Think or know?"

Preston wiggled his fingers toward Ozzy's gun. "Let me shoot Romeo. Lewis is too much of a wuss."

Lewis glared at Finn. "We might need both of them." His eyes tracked to Houston and then to Sophie. "They met with someone at the film set. They were given instructions to call a connection. I was in her horse trailer listening, but I couldn't hear it all."

Finn put his gun in his pocket, but then flicked out his knife. He stepped toward Sophie. "Can I be the one to get the information out of her?"

Houston gritted his teeth. "Don't you touch her."

Lewis stepped forward. "I know where the burner phone is that's needed for the contact."

"I ain't seen no phone. His aunt took his away because the little boy got in trouble." Preston mocked.

"Shut up, Preston. It's safe in the shed." Lewis pushed back his shoulders before he tilted his head toward Finn. "I didn't trust these two—"

Finn huffed. "That's funny coming from—"

"Enough." Ozzy snarled. "If all three of you don't grow up, I'm not keeping any of you. My cousin already thinks you're all not worthy of the cause. Preston, go with Lewy. No funny business. Just get me the phone."

As Preston passed Sophie, he grinned wickedly. "Too bad I don't have any more firecrackers, right, Mr. Hotshot?"

Finn shined his knife on his jeans and winked at Sophie. "Don't worry, after we take care of you, we'll take good care of your horses."

Sophie jumped to her feet. "Leave my horses alone. Let us go right now."

Ozzy cocked his gun.

Houston stood, and Ozzy aimed the gun at Houston's chest. "The authorities are on their way. It will go better for you if they don't find us under gunpoint."

"Good try, liar. No one is coming to save you." Ozzy chuckled. "And trust me, little Lamb. Your horses are the least of your worries. Get down. Both of you."

By the time Finn stopped laughing, Preston and Lewis reappeared from the shed. Lewis held out Crispin's phone and brought it to Ozzy, who flipped it open.

"About time you're showing your full potential." He sent a smirk in Sophie's direction. "See what happens when people give me what I want?"

"We don't have anything you need." Houston fisted the dirt beneath him. If Finn would turn back toward Houston, he could fling the dirt into the teen's eyes and tackle him. But then, he'd probably be shot by Ozzy, and that would leave Sophie more defenseless.

Lord, how will You use this for Your good?

Was there something Houston wasn't seeing?

Ozzy leveled his gaze on Lewis. "The contact we need is on this phone?"

Lewis nodded.

"Then there's no point keeping these two alive." Ozzy flicked his chin out. "Finn, you get Romeo. Preston shoots the girl."

Preston yanked Sophie's head back. At Sophie's whimper, Houston sprang up and tossed the dirt in Finn's eyes.

A gun shot ripped through the air at the same time Houston lunged for Sophie. Pain sliced through his forearm. And before he reached her, Finn tackled Houston from the side.

Houston landed on his bad hip. A moan escaped his mouth as Finn rolled into one of the tiki torches. The pole snapped. The flame fell and instantly lit a pile of dry leaves.

Dirt caked Finn's mustache as he grabbed the

broken tiki torch. "I think I'll shoot you in both legs so you can't run." He stood and touched the lit flame to more leaves on the ground. "But don't you think fire will be the perfect way for you to actually die?"

TWELVE

Sophie was not going down like this.

Not for a national security threat she had no clue about. Watching them terrorize Houston made her realize she would do anything to live—and have him in her life. Houston wasn't a liar. The sheriff was coming. But would he make it in time? There would be no hiding from the fear that clawed inside of her.

God, help me to trust You in this, too.

Fire sparked around Houston from his position on the ground. His gaze focused on Finn, who had his knife in one hand and the broken tiki torch in the other. Where was the gun Finn had? Her gaze darted from outside the fire to the ground around the hole to where Ozzy had been standing.

Ozzy had shot at Houston, but Lewis had bumped his shoulder into him, disrupting his aim. After the miss, Ozzy yelled at Lewis, and the boy had fled into the woods with his mentor roaring after.

She couldn't see either of them now, or the missing gun, with the grip Preston had on her hair and the pain that was shooting from her stitches. She needed to think.

God, help me not to be afraid of the wrong things. If You are for me...then I shouldn't fear anyone else.

She glanced over her shoulder, but no police rushed toward them. No physical rescue in sight. However, the words Houston had sung as they had gone into the fire tent captured her mind.

"Though Satan should buffet, though trials should come, let this blest assurance control. That Christ has regarded my helpless estate, and hath shed His own blood for my soul."

Peace in God was more than what she could see. More than a feeling inside of her. It was putting all her trust in the God who made all things. In good times and in tragedy.

She was so tired of running from the One who loved her.

Preston jerked once more on her ponytail. His yank brought tears to her eyes. "Don't think about moving."

Spit from his words hit the back of her neck. She tightened her fist around a handful of dirt. She inhaled another deep breath, her lungs ablaze.

Then an idea sparked. What if she didn't resist Preston's hold on her? When he tugged, she could spring back toward him and throw dirt like Houston had. Then land a punch, just like Crispin had taught her.

The fire flashed higher around Houston, who was crouched low. Had the gunshot hit him? Or was it the fire itself reminding him of the past?

God give him strength too.

He'd battled so much fire the last few days, but trauma crept back on its own timetable. Finn was inside the fire circle too and worked his way closer to

Houston. A teen or not, Finn was still armed and dangerous.

"Houston!" Sophie gasped. "Get out of there."

Preston pulled so hard on her scalp that her teeth throbbed, but this time, she didn't fight the movement. As she tipped backward, she hurled a handful of dirt toward Preston's face.

She clenched her fist, twisted her heels, and slammed a punch into his stomach. With her left hand, she raked her nails down his cheek.

Preston hollered and released her. He bent at the waist and his hands flew to his injuries.

Sophie scrambled away.

Footsteps thundered behind her.

She needed to lose Preston in the darkness of the woods. But what about Houston?

As she glanced at the pit, something shiny caught her eye. The shovel.

Three more steps and she could have a weapon of sorts.

Just two more.

Preston growled from behind her. "I'm going to kill you for making me bleed."

One last step and she grabbed the shovel handle sticking up out of the ground. Splinters jabbed her skin from the worn wood, but she only gripped it tighter.

She spun around and swung the metal blade at the same time Preston lunged.

The shovel thumped against Preston's head. It vibrated the handle, stinging Sophie's palms. She cried out.

Preston hit the dirt.

Sophie held the shovel like a baseball batter swinging for the fence.

Except Preston didn't get up.

She couldn't tell if his chest moved up and down or not, and she wasn't going to hang around long enough to wait and see. Her lungs squeezed. She couldn't stop and ponder the boy's fate until Houston was safe.

A gunshot cracked through the air.

Sophie dropped to the ground. A stick jabbed into her side. Her gaze whipped around to Houston. He hadn't been hit. Ozzy must be shooting at Lewis in the woods.

Lord, please keep the boy safe, for Marley's sake.

Houston stood with two sticks in his hands that he must have grabbed from the ground. He held them out like swords. Finn slashed toward him with his knife. Houston blocked the movement with the stick in his right hand.

Sophie sprang up, tightened her grip on the shovel, and ran. Two was better than one. She could attack Finn from behind.

But when she reached the fire, the temperature of the flames separating her from Houston and Finn hit her face. The heat made her gulp for her next breath. Her cheeks heated. Sweat dripped down her back. She had to get in there.

She tucked her chin and jumped over the two-foot flame.

Finn twisted toward her, and a gummy grin spread across his face before he spun back toward Houston. He jabbed his knife at Houston's chest.

Houston blocked the movement with the stick in his hand. Blood on his arm glistened in the firelight.

He was hurt.

Houston's gaze locked onto Sophie's. "Get out of here, Soph."

"I'm never leaving you." They would face this trial just like the others. Together.

And most importantly, not be swallowed up by the wrong type of fear. She may not always understand God's ways, but His plans were far better than anything Sophie could orchestrate on her own. She was done hiding. Done running on her own strength.

She sprinted in Finn's direction and wound back the shovel. Finn turned his knife in her direction. She swung the shovel and knocked the knife away.

Houston ran at Finn. He wrapped his arms around the teen, and as he tackled him, they both fell close to the fire.

"Houston!"

Houston locked his elbow under Finn's chin.

Finn gasped for air. His fingers clawed at Houston's arm. But the blood didn't allow Finn to get a grip on Houston.

Finally, Finn's eyes closed, and he stilled.

Houston released his hold, and Finn didn't flinch on the ground.

As Houston rushed to her, his arms circled around her. "You okay?"

Sophie nodded against his chest. "You're bleeding."

"I've survived worse. You should have left. Saved yourself."

Sophie put her palm on his chest and looked at the night's grim sky. One star slipped through the haziness. It was only one of trillions of stars. And the only One who could truly keep her safe was the Lord, who created everything. It was past time she gave Him her fears. "God didn't bring you back into my life so I could leave you alone to die."

Houston gave her his side smile. "I can't die yet. I was hoping to spend some time with you that involved less adventure and more dinner and a movie type of evening."

He tightened his hold on her and edged his chin down. His mouth came only inches from hers, but he didn't move any further.

Sophie slid her arms around him. "I'd love to spend more time with you."

Forever sounded perfect, actually. But she didn't want to scare him off with that knowledge yet.

There was no more waiting as Houston pressed his lips to hers.

She relaxed into his chest, and he wrapped her up like he never wanted to let her go. A hum of a growl came from his throat as he ended the kiss and pressed his forehead to hers. His heartbeat under her fingers seemed to gallop along with her own.

No, she didn't want to run a horse barn all by herself. She wanted to love and be loved by more than just her animals. She didn't know what the future held, but she knew she was willing to make compromises in order to have the man she had fallen in love with in it, even if that meant selling her ranch. She could have horses anywhere. But there was only one Houston. A man who not only challenged her to endure life's battles, but pointed her in the right direction with love and kindness, reminding her that there's always hope and peace in the Lord.

Houston picked something up off the ground. He extended Finn's knife. "You take this." He grabbed the shovel Sophie had left behind her. "I have to get this fire out."

Houston sank the blade of the shovel into the ground and flung the dirt on the hungry flames. Grit and determination aided his actions, not panic. He faced the fire without hesitation. He repeated the motions four times before Sophie made it to him.

"What can I do?"

As about a four-foot section of the fire had been snuffed out, Houston took her hand and led her to the other side of the flames. Now on the outside looking in, he said, "We're going to get you back to your truck and to safety."

"And leave the fire?"

Houston exhaled. "You're more important. If the crew gets here in less than thirty minutes, it shouldn't spread too much."

She glanced over the fire. It wasn't out of control. Yet.

Her eyes stopped on something black on the other side of the circle of fire. It was the discarded gun.

She rushed around Houston and picked it up. "New plan."

Kissing Sophie had been worth the wait. If only there was time to press his lips to hers again. But the woman never ceased to challenge him to do the right thing.

He nodded. As much as he wanted to get Sophie out of here, the fire wasn't something to ignore completely. "Watch for Ozzy. Call the sheriff again. If you see any burnable debris in the path of the flames, kick it away. But don't get too close. When I finish the trench around, I'll come back and stomp the fire out. Then we're out of here."

"Perfect." She pulled out her phone and kept her attention on the woods surrounding them.

Houston moved around the fire, trusting Sophie to watch his back. Finally, he scooped out the last pile to complete the trench. He turned to Sophie, who had both hands on the gun. "The fire isn't completely out, but it shouldn't go anywhere else."

The last thing the town of Ember needed was another forest fire.

He turned on his flashlight app and reached for Sophie's hand. She held tight to the gun in her other hand as she laced her left fingers with his.

After four silent steps through the dim woods, Houston asked, "Did you get hold of the sheriff?"

Sophie's next step made a leaf crunch beneath her. "Dispatch said he was on his way. Your crew as well."

"Good." He weaved around a line of trees. The old schoolhouse property should only be about fifty yards away. He could just about make out the framed outline. "That's good."

He kept his phone light steady, but there was something still making his chest squeeze. And it wasn't the gunshot that had barely sliced the top of his arm. It was not knowing where Ozzy and Lewis had gone.

"Do you think Lewis is okay?" Sophie whispered.

There had been far too much evil tonight. He hated to think the worst for the teen. "I don't know."

An owl hooted overhead. Houton paused his steps.

Sophie tugged his arm forward. "I see the dusk to

dawn light at the schoolhouse. We're almost to safety," Sophie whispered.

And that's when Ozzy's voice rang out in the darkness behind them. "Drop that gun, or I'm going to drop Romeo beside you, Ms. Lamb."

Sophie's hand shook in his palm.

"Hurry and duck behind that tree beside you," Houston breathed.

"I'm never leaving you."

Never could mean forever. He'd love to have a life with Sophie. But they couldn't do that if she wasn't safe.

The sound of Sophie dropping the gun made him tighten his grip on her.

Lord, my future's all Yours.

"Hand over the phone." Ozzy's growl came from over Houston's left shoulder.

As Houston turned, a flashlight shone in his face. Houston held out his phone.

"Is that it?" Ozzy snarled.

With a frown, Houston squinted, and that's when he noticed it was Lewis holding the light as he hid behind Ozzy, shaking his head. His face displayed three whelps. Two on either side of his cheeks. And one that already made his right eye swell shut. Ozzy had beaten the kid and yet he remained by his side.

Sophie stepped up beside Houston. "Let us go. You already have the other phone."

Houston moved in front of Sophie. But Ozzy stomped over and had them both in view. He pivoted his aim to Sophie's chest.

Houston raised his hands and slid his body closer to Sophie. "We don't have the phone. Remember, you…" He glanced at the last person to have had the phone.

Had Lewis dropped the phone and blamed them?

"That's too bad for you." Ozzy extended his gun, but before he pulled the trigger, a shout rang out behind them.

"This is the police. Put down your weapon."

Ozzy lifted his gun higher, and a shot whizzed past Houston.

Houston yanked Sophie to the ground as Ozzy grunted and grabbed his side.

As Houston checked on Sophie, Lewis screamed. "No!"

Ozzy had dropped to his knees, but his gun was locked on Sophie. Another bullet popped through the night, but this time from Ozzy's gun.

Houston lunged to cover Sophie at the same time Lewis leaped in front of Houston.

Ozzy's bullet struck Lewis's chest as another bullet flew overhead from the police.

Houston caught Lewis as Ozzy placed his hand over his heart. The gun dropped, and Ozzy collapsed to the ground.

Lewis's chest heaved, and Houston propped him up. Blood seeped into his shirt.

After everything, the boy had saved his life.

Lewis licked his lips. "S-sorry."

Houston eased Lewis to the ground and put pressure on the bleeding wound. Except the boy kept trying to move.

"I know it hurts, son, but you have to keep still."

Sophie knelt beside them. "Oh, Lewis." A hiccupped cry spilled from her mouth.

Tears filled Lewis's eyes and met Sophie's. "I-I messed up."

Houston pressed harder on the wound. Blood leaked through his fingers. "We all do. God gives forgiveness. He's the only One who can change our past and make us whole." Houston's arms shook, but he held the pressure on Lewis's wound. "He did it for me. I'd gotten in with the wrong crowd. But that didn't stop God from redeeming me."

"And me," Sophie whispered.

Physically, Lewis's body may be failing, but he still had time spiritually as long as he drew breath. "It's not too late to have your own redemption story."

Each new life for Christ mattered. This could be the very reason Houston had to endure the closed door at Last Chance County. And Lewis's eternal life would be worth it.

Lewis closed his eyes. "Sorry…" A deep gasp and then, "God."

He cried out as Houston shifted him to raise the boy's head higher than his heart. They needed to stop the blood.

Another set of hands came and lifted Lewis's head. Blood also coated the sheriff's arm and shoulder. "He saved you."

Houston readjusted his hold on the boy. "Something tells me you helped tonight too." He flicked his gaze toward Ozzy's dead body.

"Sorry it took so long." He grabbed his radio. "Get my medics back here." Then to Houston he said, "Your crew isn't far behind." He tilted his chin. "I smell smoke, but where are the flames?"

Sophie leaned against his side. "Houston trenched the fire."

Footsteps and lights were coming their way. "Sheriff?"

"Right here, Smith." The sheriff waved his flashlight.

Two men, one carrying a stretcher, sprinted over.

"We've got a male teen with a gunshot wound," the sheriff instructed.

"Finn and Preston are up that way. Though not sure if they are…" Sophie paled.

The Sheriff nodded. "I'll go check them out." After the medics bandaged Lewis, he stood. "Can you two make your way toward your vehicle and wait for me there?"

Houston held out his hand toward Sophie. She fitted her fingers around his.

The medics loaded Lewis on the board. "We're heading out with this one."

Houston stepped back, and his boot kicked against something. As the medics left, Houston kneeled and picked up what he'd kicked.

It was a phone. A tattered one.

He held it out to Sophie. "Lewis must have had Crispin's phone the entire time."

But instead of grabbing for the phone, Sophie laid her head on his shoulder. "Do you think he'll be okay?"

He didn't know if she meant her brother or Lewis. Or maybe both. Houston pressed a kiss to her forehead. "I think God still works miracles of all kinds."

Including changing Houston's stubborn heart.

Sophie turned to him and held his grimy cheeks with her dirt-lined hands. "I know He does."

Then she kissed him, and Houston found himself thankful for all of his interrupted past plans.

THIRTEEN

SOPHIE REMINDED HERSELF THAT PEOPLE HER AGE did not skip down the sidewalk. It was amazing what a good night's sleep could do. Plus, with the new day's sunshine beaming down on her face, the morning's earlier call from the bank about the barn loan's approval, and the man she was about to see, she couldn't help her smile.

Her phone rang from her pocket. She paused outside the Jude County Fire Headquarters and squinted at her new phone. Marley's name flashed on the screen.

Sophie swiped and answered. "Hey, how is Lew—"

"You at home?" Marley asked. "I have a flower order for you."

Sophie frowned at the door in front of her.

Marley kept going without a breath. "I was going to run it over before I headed back to the hospital."

"What are you doing at work?"

Marley sighed. "I needed a break from all the beeping monitors and gossip. And Betty. Lewis was sleeping, so I thought I'd grab a bite to eat."

"At work?"

"Well, why are you not at home resting like you're supposed to?" Marley countered.

Sophie wrinkled her nose. "Marley, I'm fine. Last night wasn't your fault. I promise I'm not the one you need to worry over." Plus, it had been about twelve hours since she'd seen Houston, and somehow that was already too long. "How's Lewis?"

After a moment, Marley said, "He woke up this morning and then went back to sleep. Still no problems from the surgery. They say he should recover. Finn and Preston too. There's an officer guarding their hospital rooms. I'm scared that my brother will want to lock me up in jail along with the boys for allowing his son to get into all this trouble."

"Lewis knew what he was doing was wrong," Sophie whispered. "You did your best. We tried to help him."

Marley sniffed. "I know. It still hurts though."

Sophie shifted on her feet. Her ankle was not much of an issue, and her stitches on her head no longer hurt. "I'm meeting Houston for lunch, and then I can swing by your shop and pick up the flowers…"

Hold on. If Houston was here, why would he send her flowers?

Sophie squinted back to the parking lot to where Houston's truck sat beside hers. Who else would send her something? "Marley, what does the card say?"

"Oh, well, I'd assumed Houston…hang on." A shifting of papers came over the speaker. "The invoice says three sunflowers for Sophie Lamby, huh? Maybe someone wrote your name wrong."

Lamby. "Did you say sunflowers?" Her hand went

to grasp her necklace. She pulled the rings out and stared down at the engraved sunflower on her mother's ring.

Crispin.

"I can open the card if you want."

Sophie managed a grunt that she hoped encouraged her friend. But she was pretty sure her brother was sending her a message. One that he was going to be okay.

"Finally got it open. Okay. It says...See you soon. Let's have a root beer float. My treat." Marley paused, probably flipping the card over. "There's no name. So...maybe Houston isn't great with love notes, or first date plans, but my vote is he's still a keeper."

"Thanks, Marley." Sophie choked out. "You're right. He is." Even though he wasn't the one the flowers were from. When Sophie had gotten her driver's permit, her brother had handed her the keys and said she was treating him to a root beer float for him having to teach her how to drive.

Sophie cleared her throat. "Why don't you take them to your place, and I'll swing by later and catch up. I'll grab you your favorite smoothie too."

"No, girl. I need to grab *you* a smoothie. You've been through enough."

"Doesn't mean I want to ignore your burdens. You've had a rough night too. See you at five-ish?"

Marley's sigh filled the silence. "Sounds lovely. Thanks, girl."

Sophie hung up and stepped into the headquarters. A small bench was by the front door, but laughter led her down the hall where a group of hotshots, smokejumpers, and other staff sat in a space filled with sofas and a television.

None of them were Houston.

Charlie noticed her. "Hey, Sophie."

She waved. "Do you know where…"

But the sound of a chair scooting back had Sophie looking beyond the couches and back to the long kitchen table.

Houston threw down his cards. "I fold."

Someone complained about Houston's forfeit, but Sophie couldn't take her eyes off the man who'd gone from practically an enemy to someone much more.

Houston led her out of the room and wrapped her up in a hug. He slid his fingers around hers and tugged her down the hall. He stopped just by the front bench. "Hi."

Sophie's hands were placed over his heart, right where she seemed to be planting herself. Instead of answering, she levered herself up on her toes and touched her lips to his. Once again, his arms went around her, and it felt like home.

After the sweet kiss ended, he smiled down at her. "I think I like your greeting much better than mine."

"I would offer another, but I also want to know how your meeting went this morning."

Houston took in a deep breath. "The chief wanted to rehash my hesitations."

Sophie shook her head. "You didn't hesitate last night with Finn and the fire."

He rubbed his hands up her back. "That's when I realized I no longer wanted to be a hotshot to prove myself to anyone."

She frowned. "Are you leaving Ember earlier than planned?" She had told herself that she was willing to compromise for Houston, and she still was. But it wouldn't be easy. However, he was worth it.

"We lived through so much over the last few days. I think, in the end, all of it will help me be a better hotshot. But I want to save both physical and spiritual lives. I'm thinking of applying to the open position at Ember's Community Church."

Sophie swallowed. "You're saying you want to stay in Ember?"

"Would that be awful? I think I still want to take a few seminary courses in the offseason. But probably online."

"You can stay." She tilted her head. "Only if you occasionally ride a horse now and again with me too."

He full on smirked. "Depends. Will you stick me on a horse or a mule?"

She shrugged. "I'm not picky as long as they belong to the Sunflower Ranch."

At Houston's lowered brow, she showed him the engraving on her mother's ring. "I'm thinking of renaming the ranch. The bank called on my way over, and they're letting me build another barn. I thought it would be the perfect time. Plus, sunflowers were my mother's favorite flower."

"That's perfect, Soph. Speaking of your brother's necklace...have you called his friend to pass on that message yet?"

"It took forever to charge." Sophie pulled out the phone in question from her purse. "But I wanted you with me when I did it."

Houston leaned his shoulder against the wall. "Then that's exactly where I want to be."

Sophie dialed the only person in the worn phone's contact list and put it up to her ear.

After the first ring, Houston laced his fingers through hers.

"What if no one answers?" Sophie asked. "We won't be able to—"

Someone else in the hallway jogged toward them. "Excuse me, James."

The voice had both Houston and Sophie moving closer to the bench so the striking smokejumper coming down the hall could get past them to the exit. "Sorry, Booth."

At the third ring, Sophie's stomach squeezed. "Should I—"

"Hello?" a man answered.

Sophie gripped the phone. "Yes, hi. Umm…" What was she supposed to say again?

"I think you have the wrong—"

"I don't have the wrong number." She took a breath. "Crispin needed you to know that the brothers are back. No, that wasn't what he said." She squeezed the bridge of her nose. "It's the brothers are *here*."

After three heartbeats, the male voice lowered. "Who is this? How do you know Crispin? Wait, he's *alive*?"

Sophie opened her mouth, but the presence of Houston's fingers squeezing around hers reminded her that it wasn't only her safety that could be in danger if she gave away too much info.

But also, the man she'd fallen in love with.

She ended the call, hanging up on Crispin's colleague. Her brother hadn't wanted the man on the other side of the phone to know anything more. She pressed her shoulder against Houston. He simply held her, and that was exactly what she needed.

"You're a good sister." He ran his fingers through the ends of her hair. "You did what you said you would."

"*We* did what *we* said *we* would. Isn't there a famous saying about once lab partners always lab partners?"

"Even if there isn't,"—he lifted her hand off his chest and kissed the back of it—"I like the idea of always with you."

All too soon, he sighed. "I know I said eleven o'clock, but can you wait a bit longer? It's about time for our briefing."

"Of course. I'll wait." She lowered herself to the bench in the hallway.

Houston turned to Sophie. "Soph, after everything…are you sure you're okay with my job? I mean, I would do something else…"

He didn't have to finish his sentence. She understood. He was willing to compromise for her too.

She smiled up at her handsome hero. "I couldn't think of a better hotshot."

He walked toward his crew but glanced back. "At lunch, maybe you could ask me again if I'm happy." He winked right before he rounded the corner.

Sophie grinned. The last time she'd asked him if he was happy was after she had tightened her seatbelt while they were chasing Lewis. That seemed like a lifetime ago. Each twist and turn of their past had molded them.

They would still face trials, but even through life's flames, God's plans always led to His hope and perfect peace.

A NOTE FROM MEGAN

Dear Reader,

When I was little, I'd often announce to my mom that I was going outside to run. And strangely, I would. Up and down our sidewalk. Then, in junior high, I discovered running hurdles. Earning blue and red ribbons on the track team was so much fun. However, during one race, I fell. *Hard*. I shoved myself up and got back into the race. I jumped the next hurdle only to trip over another. There would be no third try that night. I twisted my ankle. Scraped up my shoulder, palms, and knees. Yet all the bruises and physical pain weren't the worst of it. I soon healed and raced again. But now, there was a fear. The memory of pain. The falls. The failure. Ever on my mind as my legs would tremble in the starting blocks with my gaze locked on the now seemingly mountainous hurdles before me.

Life, too, beats us up sometimes, doesn't it? We hurdle over trials only to find evil and difficulties everywhere. We fall or get pushed down by stresses, worries, and hardships. Fear enters, and soon, we're at the end of our strength.

My book, *Flashover*, goes along with the second verse of the hymn, "It Is Well." *"Though Satan should buffet, though trials should come, let this blest assurance control. That Christ has regarded my helpless estate, and hath shed His own blood for my soul."*

Sophie and Houston had their fair share of obstacles, and some of them weren't caused by their own doing; rather a result of someone else's sin. But amongst the chaos, did you notice the water tower early in the book? It was often in the main character's view just up ahead. And then, when things for Houston and Sophie were at their worst—the flashover, which basically means things explode—the water tower poured out, bringing victory.

Oh, how Jesus—the Living Water—loves us. He is far better than any water tower. He knows how helpless we truly are, and through the shedding of His blood, He offers us redemption and hope in Him.

At the start, Sophie was running in fear and desperation. She didn't want to repeat her past hurts, but she galloped forward with her own strength. While Houston had set his sights on his own plans, not the Lord's.

The only saving path is Christ. Not the directions of our own plans or worldly so-called securities. Proverbs 18:10 says, "The name of the Lord is a strong tower; the righteous run to it and are safe."

In this world, I sure need a strong tower. Does this mean all our troubles are over when we run to Him? No, but under His care we are now comforted with His joy and peace. Oh, dear reader, it can be well with our souls. We must take our eyes off life's hurdles and fears before us and run to Jesus.

Why jump and fall in this life, when He can carry us through.

With love and prayers,

Megan Besing

ACKNOWLEDGMENTS

To my Lord and Savior. You are so good. From the spark of a story idea to the pit of my overflowing to-do list, may I always fully cling to You. I pray that my life and all the words on these pages bring You honor and glory. Thank You for Your forgiveness, love, and faithfulness. And thanks for carrying me through the month of September. (Actually, for all the months. But You get it.)

To my husband. My love, thanks for your love and support. THANK YOU for making dinner when I was trying to quite chaotically juggle our lives, teaching, and my story worlds. And to my kids, thanks for embracing your mother's weirdness. Do you want a hug? How about now? P.S. Love you, both. Always.

Abigail Wilson, thank you for your friendship and for your encouragement with not only writing but all that life includes. #youareablessing #iheartyou And I still wish you lived closer.

To my family—Including All. My. In-Laws—thanks for your love and support and pointing me to Jesus. For feeding me! And Mom, thanks for speaking book talk with me.

Laura Conaway, thanks for your prayers and sharing in this writing adventure. I am blessed by your friendship.

And Erin Smithers, I appreciate your Godly

council and reminders to dig into God's Truth, which not only helps me grow spiritually but also as a result, strengthens the Spiritual threads in my stories.

Thanks to Luke (and Karlee) for answering my questions about electrotherapy. I hope I made Houston's story all that it should have been.

Thank you, Rachel Kent. You are the best agent. Seriously. I'm honored to be represented by you and Books and Such.

Susan May Warren, Lisa Phillips, and the entire Sunrise team, thank you for making my stories so much better and for all that you do.

To my new fellow teachers, thank you for morning devotions time. Thank you for lifting up in prayer my creative endeavors despite not understanding all that it includes. It is a joy to work with you all.

And to my readers. THANK YOU. Thanks for cheering on me and my stories. I appreciate you so much! Please come say hi on social media. You'll make my day.

Thank you for reading *Flashover*! Gear up for the next
Chasing Fire: Montana romantic suspense thriller,
Flashback by Michelle Sass Aleckson. Keep reading
for a sneak peek!

**SECRETS. BETRAYAL. SACRIFICE.
THIS TIME, THEY'RE NOT JUST
FIGHTING FIRE.**

CHASING FIRE: MONTANA | BOOK 3

FLASH BACK

A SERIES CREATED BY
SUSAN MAY WARREN
& LISA PHILLIPS

MICHELLE SASS ALECKSON
PUBLISHERS WEEKLY BESTSELLING AUTHOR

He's the last person she wants to see...
  Allie Monroe is desperate for a fresh start.

Grieving the loss of her first SAR dog, she's gone to Montana to train her new K9, Scout. And when two boys go missing during a wildfire, she's brought on board to find them.

But the one person tasked to help her is the *last* person she wants to see—arrogant and dangerous Dakota Masterson.

It'll take exactly this man to save everything she loves.

Former SWAT officer Dakota Masterson is a new man after confronting the demons of his past, including his first unfortunate meeting with Allie. But admittedly, she's the last person he thought he'd see again...or have to work with. Still, maybe this is his chance to prove to her that he's a different man—because she's the one woman he can't seem to forget.

However, with the flames closing in, finding the boys might mean confronting the painful memories of their short-lived relationship. Then, Allie's dog goes missing, suddenly someone is shooting at them, and they find themselves in a race against a wildfire and a threat that wants them dead. More, when Allie goes missing, Dakota's past—and his issues—come roaring back.

It'll take the SWAT officer in him to save the day, but will it cost them a future they both long for?

Get ready to be swept away in a world where survival, redemption, and second chances collide in book three of the Chasing Fire: Montana series.

FLASHBACK

CHASING FIRE: MONTANA | BOOK 3

CHAPTER 1

These mountains were Allie Monroe's last hope. They weren't nearly far enough to escape her past, but then again, nothing was. At least here she had the best shot at getting away and focusing on her search and rescue work. It's really all she had, and she'd been out of it for far too long. She'd settle for a good training session with Scout so she could get back to it.

Of course, to do that, her best friend needed to get out of her cozy little bed in the camper next door. Allie might not be able to see the sun dawning on the horizon, with all the trees and the Rocky Mountains in the way, but there was plenty of light to hit the forest trail, even with the haze of wildfire smoke in the air.

Her phone rang. Allie stared at the picture of her mother and father together right outside the church she'd grown up in. Their smiling faces stirred up too much to deal with this early in the morning. She'd have to call her mother later. Or text. Mom would understand. There was too much riding on getting

Scout trained to hear all about how great her siblings were doing at the moment.

She set the prepped backpack by her orange-and-yellow tent while her black Labrador sniffed around the campsite. He followed his nose to the base of a ponderosa pine until the slap of the camper door broke his concentration. He made a beeline for Belle Jamison as she walked toward them.

Finally.

"Ugh. How do you function this early?" Belle's blonde curls escaping from the wide floral headband took the term *bed head* to a new level.

"You're awake." Allie pocketed her phone. "Great. I was thinking—"

"Whoa. Pump the brakes." Belle held up a hand. "I'm here, but I need a shower house visit and a couple mugs of coffee before I'm ready for anything."

Scout whined. Her friend knelt down and scrubbed his neck with both hands. His tail thumped like a jackhammer.

"He's a morning person like you." Belle's groggy voice teased. "No wonder you picked him out."

"Actually, Dani picked him out for me." As one of the lead trainers at the SAR K9 school outside of Benson, Washington, Dani Masterson was who Allie aspired to be. "He's smart, but he's no Dixie. He hardly listens to me on the first go."

"Yeah, but is it even fair to compare the two dogs?"

"I guess not." No animal could replace the sweet golden retriever mix that had stayed loyally by her side for the last seven years. Dixie could practically read her mind.

"You and Dixie just had a special bond. You'll get there with Scout too."

Would she? Her bond with Dixie had been forged by heartbreak and trauma, and even Belle didn't know the whole of it. Allie couldn't go through that again.

She shook the painful memories away.

Scout was intelligent and eager. He had the drive a search and rescue K9 needed, but they still weren't...connecting.

"He needs to trust me. And we should've been at that point months ago."

"Give him time." Belle stood, letting Scout go on exploring. "And I know that's why you're all gung ho about hitting the trail and getting that training done, so why don't you brew us some coffee and I'll be back in a jiff." She walked away toward the shower house in her flip-flops and pajama shorts.

Right. Coffee. And probably she should feed her dog. "Scout, come."

He glanced her way for a second, then went back to sniffing out what was probably a chipmunk trail. He lifted a back leg and left his mark.

"Gee, thanks." She stifled the sigh that rose. How exactly did Dani get him to listen to her? She could whisper a command at the training school, and Scout would immediately follow it and beg for more.

She tried a slightly higher voice. "Ready for breakfast?"

At that, she had all his attention. Scout trotted over and sat at her feet.

"Oh, sure. You come on the first call if it's got to do with food, huh?"

She scooped food into his collapsible camping

bowl. "Eat up now. As soon as Belle is back and properly caffeinated, she'll hide out in that big forest, and you get to find her."

He didn't bother looking up at her as he dug into his kibble.

"I know you hear me." She just didn't understand why he didn't *listen* to her. They needed that figured out by the end of this five-day trip.

She'd already missed so many opportunities. Opportunities to help find the lost. God couldn't possibly expect her to sit around doing nothing while she had the resources to help.

It was going to be a hot one though. Even in her light trail pants and moisture-wicking tee, she was sweating. The air was heavy with smoke. She'd had to fight to find a cancellation to get this spot when she'd reserved it last month, but a good chunk of the campsites remained empty now, thanks to a wildfire outside of Ember. It had already burned hundreds of acres, but it seemed to be contained for the moment, according to the last report she'd found. It kept her friend Emily Micah, a hotshot firefighter, too busy to meet up with, but that was okay since Allie was here to train Scout.

He finished his breakfast and went back to sniffing around the trees.

Allie dug through her supply tote for the percolator and coffee grounds.

"Nice doggie!" A little boy in a striped shirt and floppy-rimmed explorer hat left the campground gravel road and crossed the sandy dirt to approach her useless campfire ring. With the burn ban, it was propane fuel only for heating up her water.

He reached out to pet Scout.

"Nolan, you shouldn't pet a strange dog without asking." An older boy—probably a brother, given the similar blue eyes and tawny blond hair—pulled the younger one away.

Allie smiled at the boys. "It's okay. You can introduce yourselves if you like. Let him smell you." The boys moved closer. Allie knelt by Scout and held his collar. "This is Scout and I'm Allie."

Nolan squatted in front of Scout, who proceeded to lick a sticky purple smear off the boy's cheek. The older brother stuck a hand out in Allie's direction. "I'm Ethan. This is my brother Nolan."

Allie shook the proffered hand. "Nice to meet you."

"We're here for the weekend. We're over there with the blue tent." He pointed a few spots down the way with a black truck parked next to the metal fire ring.

"And where are you off to so early? You look like you're ready for an adventure." Their tent was zipped up, no adults in sight.

"We wanna get another hike in before we hafta go home."

"Alone?" The older boy could've been nine or ten, but his younger brother looked like he was barely in kindergarten.

"We've been here a bunch of times. I keep Nolan safe. And we always have our survival packs." He pointed to his rather full backpack.

"What about your parents? Do they know you're going on a hike?"

Ethan balked. "Of course my mom knows. We do this all the time."

Nolan stopped petting Scout long enough to nod.

"That's pretty...brave."

Ethan pulled his shoulders back and puffed out his chest a little.

"Ethan knows these trails real good. And he is super-duper brave. Like when we hided and runned away from that bad man, or when Ray tells scary stories about grizzly bears or ghosts. He never gets scared." Nolan moved over and grinned up at his big brother.

But wait—

"A bad man? On the trail?" Allie asked them.

Ethan elbowed his little brother. "He's just making that up. Like the ghost stories. Right, Nolan?"

Nolan's face scrunched up. "We saw that scary—"

"Bear. Yeah, we saw the bear, but it was a black bear. Not a grizzly. And it was far away." Ethan backed away, pulling Nolan with him. "We better go if we want to do the Green Hiking Loop. Mom said we're leaving after lunch. And you know Ray hates it if we're late."

Something flashed in the little boy's eyes, but it dissolved into giggles when Scout gave him one more lick. "Okay. Bye, Scout! I'll come say goodbye before we go home!"

The boys skipped off in the hazy air. Oh, to be carefree and excited like a child. Following the siren call of adventure and imagination only caused trouble. Trouble she was still paying for every day.

But she wasn't their parent.

And didn't that send a shaft of pain straight to her heart.

If their mother was okay with them hiking alone, hopefully they'd be all right. But she couldn't quite settle the unease in her middle as she watched them go off down the gravel road.

The Green Hiking Loop.

Maybe that's where they should do their training this morning. Just in case.

Allie went back to her burner and lit the blue flame under the percolator.

"I hope my boys weren't bothering you." The woman who walked into Allie's campsite was young and pretty, with wavy brunette hair pulled back in a ponytail and dark brown eyes. Eyes acquainted with hardship, giving her an older appearance.

Because of Ray and his scary stories, maybe?

"Ethan and Nolan? They just wanted to meet Scout here." Allie nodded toward the Lab, who had already trotted over to the woman and sniffed her boots. "They weren't a bother."

"Good."

"I'm Allie."

The woman made no move to come closer, keeping her gaze directed at Scout and offering him some scratches behind the ears. He leaned into her legs as if he couldn't get enough.

Huh. He never did that for Allie.

Even a perfect stranger had a better bond with her dog. But who was she?

"What's your name again?" Allie asked.

"Oh, I'm Jen." She didn't quite meet Allie's eyes as she gave a tremulous smile in her direction. Must be shy. Her boys certainly weren't though.

"So, the boys were off to hike the Green Loop. They must be pretty experienced to go by themselves."

"They're in Boy Scouts. They know these trails

since we're here so often. I can hardly keep up with them anymore."

"You're not afraid of wild animals or something happening to them? I'm an SAR worker, so I get a little paranoid, I admit. But they mentioned a scary man."

Jen's eyes widened for a nanosecond. It was so slight Allie almost didn't see it as Jen quickly laughed and waved her hand, as if pushing Allie's concern aside. "Oh, the boys love telling stories. I blame my husband. He's always riling them up with ghost stories and the like. They always try to outdo him. And they have such vivid imaginations at this age."

But following a flight of fancy could have dangerous consequences. How could this woman so flippantly let the boys go gallivanting off in the woods?

Hopefully Belle would be back soon, and they wouldn't be too far behind the boys.

Before she could ask anything more, Jen stuffed her hands in her jean pockets. "I better get back. We leave soon, and it's easier to pack everything without the boys' help."

She gave a half-hearted smile and walked away. Walked away in her dark jeans and a flannel shirt, while Allie was ready to rip off her trail pants and trade them for shorts, except that she didn't want to deal with the mosquito bites, scratches, or ticks once they were in the forest.

"Scout, come." She snapped her fingers.

The Lab looked at her but then focused once more on the woman walking away. Allie called again, this time a little more gusto in the command. Scout whined but obeyed. He was acting strange, even for him. Allie absently stroked his ears as she watched Jen reach her own site.

"Look at you making friends." Belle walked up, hair still wet, but she was dressed for the day in leggings and a long-sleeve tee. "Who was that?"

"Just another camper. Her boys wanted to meet Scout. But she's letting them hike all alone." Allie turned down the flame as the coffee inside bubbled. "I thought we could use the same trail for training this morning. In case they run into trouble."

"Give me some of that coffee you have there, and we can get started."

Belle's phone rang. By the way her eyes lit, it had to be her husband, Matthew. She stepped over toward her camper and answered. Allie focused on the coffee, trying not to eavesdrop on the newlyweds. She tamped down the irritation at yet another delay. She should be grateful she was even able to convince Belle to come with her for the trip when she'd barely left Matthew's side since the wedding four months ago. But if it was anything like every other phone conversation they'd had, Allie might as well settle in for the long haul.

She glanced at Allie with a forced smile and then pointed toward her camper. "But we just got here last night," Belle said. The door slapped shut behind her.

Yup. This was going to be a while.

But it was only a few minutes before Belle was walking out of the camper with worry lines on her forehead.

"What's going on?" Allie handed her friend a mug of coffee.

"We need to go." Belle sipped her drink.

"I know. As soon as you finish, we can." Allie whistled to Scout. It took three times, but he finally came and sat at her feet. Reluctantly.

"No, Al. We need to leave. Matthew said that wildfire is too close. He's not comfortable with us being out here."

"But I thought the fire was to the east. I checked yesterday."

Belle shook her head slowly. "It's heading this way. According to what Matt's buddies at the fire department said, he's surprised they haven't issued an evacuation order yet."

"If they haven't issued the order yet, we're fine."

"Maybe, but I told Matt I'd head home today."

"Belle—"

"If he were here and I was back home, I'd want him to leave. I think you and Scout should leave too."

"Leave? Now? We just got here yesterday." She needed training time. This was her chance.

"Why don't you come to Idaho with me? You could see our new place. You haven't been back to Twin Valley in ages."

And be a jolly third wheel to the honeymoon couple? As much as she missed Belle and was happy for her to have found true love, she didn't think she could stomach five days of witnessing their happy lives together and all that Allie would never experience herself. And besides, she couldn't leave knowing the boys were out in the Kootenai National Forest alone.

"Go ahead, Belle. But Scout and I will stay." Allie opened up her backpack, looking for Scout's harness.

"Don't be like that. There's plenty of wilderness where I am—"

"You need to be with Matthew. I get that. But I can't go. Not yet." Allie slipped Scout's harness on him, focusing on the clip, willing her eyes not to drip the tears stinging them. This was supposed to be time with her best friend. Time together and time to figure out how to get Scout to listen to her.

"Allie, you don't have to do this alone."

"I'm not alone. I have Scout." Allie stood and settled her backpack straps onto her shoulders. She dug up a bright smile for her friend. "It's okay. We'll just stay a day or two, and maybe I'll stop and see you on my way home."

Belle studied her as if sniffing out any sign of caving. With a resigned sigh, her brow relaxed. "Are you sure?"

"Those boys are still out there, and Scout knows their scent. That will be our training today. And if there's any sign of the fire getting close, I'll leave. But for now, I'll stay, and we'll be fine." Allie gave Belle a squeeze. "Really."

"Maybe this will be good. You could hike this morning for fun. Get some *bonding* time with Scout."

Allie quirked an eyebrow. "What exactly are you implying?"

"It's just...I've seen you with Scout now, and I don't think he has a listening problem. I think you two haven't bonded yet, and it's because you're holding back."

Allie folded her arms across her chest. "I have spent every waking hour of the last few months with that dog."

211

Belle didn't stand down. She met Allie's stare-down with a pointed look of her own. "You spend a lot of time with him, yes. But you barely touch him. You talk to him only when it's something you need him to do. And I haven't seen you once smile or look at him like you actually like him. Like you would with Dixie—"

"Let's not go there." Allie clenched her teeth together tight, willing the emotions clogging her throat to stay down and not leak out.

Belle must've gotten the message. "So you're not ready to talk about that. Fine. But I'm here for you when you are." She wrapped her arms around Allie's stiff shoulders. "Al, come with me. Please."

Allie allowed herself to relax a fraction and lean into her friend's embrace. "I love you, Belle, but you belong with Matthew." And she belonged...well, nowhere, really. Not that she had anyone but herself to blame. "You should get going." She pulled away and stood tall.

"What about your family? They miss you."

"I talk to them all the time." With her six siblings, it tended to be more texts, but still. She stayed in touch. "Mom and Dad call weekly."

"Calls that I've heard tend to go to voicemail or are cut short."

"I can't help that they always call while I'm busy."

"Which is exactly why you should come with me. You can have some quality time with me *and* your parents."

"My job is riding on this. I have to stay."

"There's nothing I can say that will convince you to leave?"

"You know me better than that." Allie tried on a smirk. She didn't need Belle worrying about her.

Belle chuckled as she rolled her eyes. "Yeah, I do. But first, I think I have enough time to cook you a real breakfast instead of one of those gross protein bars you're so fond of."

As much as she wanted to hit the trail, she wouldn't begrudge one last meal with her BFF.

They lingered over their pancakes and bacon—Belle always did have a knack for pancakes—but eventually Allie helped her friend unhook the lines to the camper and pack her little Subaru.

Belle headed toward Allie's tent. "We should get you packed up and ready to go."

More delays. "That's okay. You should hit the road. I know Matthew is texting you."

Belle's sheepish grin said she'd guessed right. "Yeah, but you helped me. I can—"

"It's a little tent. It won't take long. You should get back to your husband." Allie steered Belle toward the car.

"All right. But promise me you will get everything ready. And you'll come visit me on your way to Benson."

"Of course."

Allie pushed away the disappointment of the ruined trip and put on as cheerful a face as she could muster to wave goodbye when Belle pulled out. True to her word, she took her own tent down and packed all her belongings in her SUV.

Finally, she clipped the lead on Scout's harness, ready to track the two boys on the Green Hiking Loop. They were probably back by now, but Scout could still follow their trail.

"Come on, Scout. Let's go for a hike."

She took two steps before a fire truck pulled into the campground, lights flashing.

A loud voice from a speaker called out. "This is Jude County Hotshots. Please evacuate the campground as quickly and safely as possible."

Looking for more more exciting romantic suspense from Sunrise Publishing?

DON'T MISS ANY CHASING FIRE: MONTANA STORIES

With heart-pounding excitement, gripping suspense, and sizzling (but clean!) romance, the CHASING FIRE: MONTANA series, brought to you by the incredible authors of Sunrise Publishing, including the dynamic duo of bestselling authors Susan May Warren and Lisa Phillips, is your epic summer binge read.

Immerse yourself in a world of short, captivating novels that are designed to be devoured in one sitting. Each book is a standalone masterpiece, (no story cliffhangers!) although you'll be craving the next one in the series!

Follow the Montana Hotshots and Smokejumpers as they chase a wildfire through northwest Montana. The pages ignite with clean romance and high-stakes danger—these heroes (and heroines!) will capture your heart. The biggest question is...who will be your summer book boyfriend?

ELITE GUARDIANS: SAVANNAH

Safety. Secrets. Sacrifice. What will it cost these Elite Guardians to protect the innocent? Discover the answers in our Elite Guardians: Savannah series.

SCAN OUR QR CODE FOR MORE ROMANTIC SUSPENSE!

ABOUT MEGAN BESING

Despite adoring happily-ever-afters, **Megan Besing** didn't unlock a love for reading until her mid-twenties, which quickly expanded into writing. Her stories have won many awards, but her most cherished achievements are being a wife and mother. She lives in a pocket-size Indiana town, centered around extended family. She's always planning a road trip with a view, yet her favorite place may just be on her front porch drinking tea.

Connect with Megan at **meganbesing.com**.

- facebook.com/MeganBesingWriter
- instagram.com/meganbesing
- x.com/MeganBesing
- bookbub.com/authors/megan-besing
- goodreads.com/meganbesing
- amazon.com/stores/Megan-Besing/author/B073X2W8CV

ALSO BY MEGAN BESING

ROMANTIC SUSPENSE

Expired Hope

HISTORICAL ROMANCE

The Rancher's Want Ad Mix Up

The Mail-Order Brides Collection

CONNECT WITH SUNRISE

Thank you again for reading *Flashover.* We hope you enjoyed the story. If you did, would you be willing to do us a favor and leave a review? It doesn't have to be long—just a few words to help other readers know what they're getting. (But no spoilers! We don't want to wreck the fun!) Thank you again for reading!

We'd love to hear from you—not only about this story, but about any characters or stories you'd like to read in the future. Contact us at www.sunrisepublishing.com/contact.

We also have a monthly update that contains sneak peeks, reviews, upcoming releases, and fun stuff for our reader friends. Sign up at www.sunrisepublishing.com or scan our QR code.

MORE EPIC ROMANTIC ADVENTURE

CHASING FIRE: MONTANA

Flashpoint by Susan May Warren
Flashover by Megan Besing
Flashback by Michelle Sass Aleckson
Firestorm by Lisa Phillips
Fireline by Kate Angelo
Fireproof by Susan May Warren

MONTANA FIRE BY SUSAN MAY WARREN

Where There's Smoke (Summer of Fire)
Playing with Fire (Summer of Fire)
Burnin' For You (Summer of Fire)
Oh, The Weather Outside is Frightful (Christmas novella)
I'll be There (Montana Fire/Deep Haven crossover)
Light My Fire (Summer of the Burning Sky)
The Heat is On (Summer of the Burning Sky)
Some Like it Hot (Summer of the Burning Sky)
You Don't Have to Be a Star (spin-off)

LAST CHANCE FIRE AND RESCUE BY LISA PHILLIPS

Expired Return
Expired Hope (with Megan Besing)

LAST CHANCE COUNTY BY LISA PHILLIPS